NEVER

A LONG STORY

NEVER A LONG STORY

Love, Loss, Murder & More

PRABHAT PODDAR

AMARYLLIS
An imprint of Manjul Publishing House

AMARYLLIS
An imprint of Manjul Publishing House Pvt. Ltd.
• C-16, Sector 3, Noida, Uttar Pradesh 201 301, India
Website: www.manjulindia.com
Registered Office:
• 2nd Floor, Usha Preet Complex, 42 Malviya Nagar,
Bhopal 462 003 – India
Distribution Centres
Ahmedabad, Bengaluru, Chennai, Hyderabad,
Kochi, Kolkata, Mumbai, Noida, Pune

Never A Long Story: Love, Loss, Murder & More by Prabhat Poddar

This paperback edition first published in India in 2026

ISBN 978-93-7317-817-2

Cover design: Habib Ali

Printed and bound in India by Repro India Limited

To God, my family, friends and everyone who has ever shown me kindness.

Author's Note

I always wanted to be a filmmaker, but didn't know how. I thought maybe writing stories could become the bridge between where I was and where I wanted to be.

But slowly, writing stories became my escape from daily pressures. It gave me the kind of relief nothing else did, and the joy of cracking a story and writing it – to just the right climax – became my happy time.

I loved to experiment while writing these stories, and if my friends enjoyed one of them, it gave me a dopamine rush. I hope you'll enjoy reading them as much as I enjoyed writing them.

Contents

1

THE CAFÉ STORY

It's never easy to follow your parents' advice—even more difficult when you know they're right.

Oh, sorry! I forgot to introduce myself. I'm Nidhi Sharma, twenty-four years old—independent, charming, and frustrated. Why? Because my parents have achieved their first moral victory over me today: they've managed to convince me to meet some guy they deem fit for me to marry.

Of course, I didn't agree in the beginning, so they launched an all-out attack on my freedom with statements like, 'What kind of fool are you not to marry at this age?' or 'What will happen to you after we're gone?'

But I defended myself with replies like, 'It's my life, Dad!'

Then my parents changed tack and began their guerrilla warfare *tactics*. I couldn't survive the bombardment of their tears and emotional dialogues like, 'It's the only hope your old parents have left,' or 'All every parent wants is their child's happiness.'

Although they'd never seen him—and neither had I—

his impressive *biodata* was apparently sufficient. So here I was, heading towards my *destination destruction*.

The boy I was supposed to meet was one *Saahil Dwivedi*—working for his father's business and having all the so-called qualities of a good husband.

Although my parents aren't conservative and have given me enough freedom to choose someone I like, traditional Indian values have their own way of showing up in your already complicated life. So, just to make them happy, I agreed to this meeting. You can waste three hours for your parents' sake, after all. And who knows—maybe the restaurant serves great desserts.

The waiter led me to the reserved table. The man sitting there was nowhere close to handsome; he was just... okay. Well-dressed and well-mannered, though. But honestly, all boys behave well when they meet their prospective wives—and so do girls.

Nidhi: 'I'm sorry, I think I'm late.'

Saahil: 'Well, you couldn't be more right.'

What a jerk! Please take back my comment about him being well-mannered.

Nidhi: 'Uh... sorry again, but you know traffic—you just can't rely on it.'

Saahil: 'You're right again; that's why people nowadays leave early for appointments.'

Nidhi: 'Wow, are you always like this, or are you actually enjoying insulting me?'

Saahil: 'People don't like to hear the truth. They'd rather settle for deception. You're just taking my honesty as rudeness.'

Nidhi: 'But there should be some respect when you talk to a woman.'

Saahil: 'I don't know why women demand special treatment in softer matters but want equal status in everything else.'

Nidhi: 'Probably you wouldn't understand—it's a *gentlemanly thing* to do.'

Saahil: 'Hahaha, crap—nothing but hypocrisy. If I do what you want, I'm a gentleman; if I show you the watch, I'm suddenly an unworthy human being. You think I'll agree to that? No way. If women are weak, they should accept that. And if they believe they're strong, they should deal with the situation themselves.'

Nidhi: 'Okay, okay, I give up. Hey, what were you doing—writing something?' *(She points to a paper in front of him.)*

Saahil: 'Yeah, I was writing a romantic poem. Then I saw you, and the whole inspiration vanished.'

Nidhi: 'You are such an asshole! Why do you even think for a second that a girl would say yes to marrying you?'

Saahil: 'Frankly, Nidhi, I don't care. You weren't in my life a few minutes ago, and I was fine. Now we've met, and most probably we'll never meet again—and I'll still live the same life. You get what I mean?'

Nidhi: 'So... you mean you're rejecting me?'

Saahil: 'That thought never crossed my mind. I presume it'll be *your* decision.'

Nidhi: 'So you think I'm going to reject you?'

Saahil: 'Of course—you look sensible enough to comprehend the situation.'

Nidhi: 'I don't know what to say. Either you have very high confidence or very low self-esteem—maybe both.'

Saahil: '*Practical* might be the word you're looking for. With a face like mine, girls rarely appreciate the kind of humour I've got.'

Nidhi: 'My God, you really believe that? Girls don't go for looks; they care about the man who's beautiful on the inside.'

Saahil gave Nidhi a strange look and laughed.

Saahil: 'Aren't we the romantic type!'

Nidhi: 'Come on, tell me—haven't you ever had a girlfriend? Some girl must've found your style amusing.'

Saahil: 'I'll tell you a secret, Nidhi. Girls can't handle the truth. They want to be pampered. If you tell the ugliest girl she's the "lifeline of the town", she'll believe you—because she *wants* to believe it. But if someone tells her the truth, she'll break his head. And the problem is, the only thing I offer is the truth.'

The statement took Nidhi by surprise. Saahil was right—women did have their weaknesses.

Saahil: 'It's not like I never found a girl attractive. But I learned their feelings for me the hard way. Sometimes it was the regular stuff like "We're just friends," or "I never saw you that way," or even the classic—"I consider you a brother." Hahaha. I know the kind of guys they *don't* call brother—the ones who smoke, drink for fashion, and avoid commitment. But girls think they can *change* such guys. It becomes an ego issue—to turn a rebel into a tame dog. And in the end, they realise they've failed miserably. Remember this, girl: *men never change*.

'Guys like me? We're just the backup option—reliable and available when the "love of their life" rejects them.'

Nidhi reflected for a few seconds. She could recall three

boys she'd found attractive—and two who'd liked her—and how all those stories ended the same way.

Nidhi: 'So you mean there's no hope for guys like you?'

Saahil: 'It's miserable to chase girls hoping for attention and getting sympathy instead. I believe in winning or losing, not in consolation prizes. I really loved a girl once. Thought I had a chance. But I was never even her *second* option. Tell me, you wouldn't have come for this meeting if you'd found someone of your choice, right?'

Well, it was true. Nidhi had broken up recently—and this meeting was really just a distraction.

Nidhi: 'So how did you deal with it when she said no?'

Saahil: 'There wasn't much I could do except deal with it. It kills you to let go of someone you love—and even more to realise she never liked you back. All you can do in the end is either cry or laugh over your misfortune.'

Nidhi: 'I never thought you were this sensitive, Mr Dwivedi.'

Saahil: 'Neither did I—until I fell in love.'

They sat in silence for a while until Nidhi spoke again.

Nidhi: 'It's been more than three months since my breakup—but lately, I've started to come to terms with it.'

Saahil: 'Hahaha, really? I bet you still count the days. How many has it been?'

Nidhi: 'Ninety-seven. How far did you count?'

Saahil: 'Till one twenty-eight, I think.'

Nidhi: 'So, thirty-one more days to go, I suppose.' (Both laugh)

Nidhi: 'So, we share a common background, then. It actually feels good to share something I hadn't shared with anyone for the last ninety-seven days. (Some more laughter)

Nidhi: 'You know, you're really a nice guy, Saahil.'

Saahil: 'You know, that's exactly what she said when she dumped me.'

Nidhi: 'Well, I'm not going to do that. I actually find you amusing—and probably you have what I never found in any guy before: honesty. Insulting, yes—but bearable.'

Saahil (softly): 'Nidhi, I have a confession to make. I'm not Saahil Dwivedi. My actual name is Arvind. I'm Saahil's friend. He sent me here to destroy any chance of this meeting turning into something serious.'

Nidhi: 'What the f***?! What do you mean? Oh my God—that's why we never got your photo! But why would he do that?'

Arvind: 'Just like you, he was being forced by his parents. And, as luck would have it, he hadn't broken up with his girlfriend yet. So, he thought saying no to you would be the sensible thing to do.'

Nidhi: 'But why *you*? He could have done this himself.'

Arvind: 'Hahaha, he thinks I'm good at this. I've got an impeccable record of repelling girls—just by my presence.'

Nidhi: 'So all the things you said—you didn't mean any of it?'

Arvind: 'On the contrary, I've never been more honest. My friend told me to be myself. I'm sorry I lied about my name, but not about anything else.'

Nidhi: 'Well, I never thought this meeting would end this way.'

Arvind: 'Nor did I. Please don't tell your parents about

this—otherwise Saahil's parents will find out too, and that won't help anyone. Maybe if we'd met under different circumstances, then maybe... Sorry, I shouldn't have said that.'

Nidhi: 'Okay—just tell me the time and place.'

Arvind: 'What do you mean?'

Nidhi: 'I'm giving you a chance to meet me under *different circumstances.*'

Arvind: 'Wait—you mean you're actually interested in me?'

Nidhi: 'Well, I don't know what *you* understood—I can't be more explicit than that. I need to meet Arvind officially. Otherwise, how will I explain to my parents why I want to marry *Arvind* when I went to meet *Saahil?*'

2

CRIME IN PROGRESS

(i)

Hi, I am Dinkar Joshi, and crime is my business!

Although I am not a criminal—just a crime-fiction writer, or rather an upcoming (read: unknown) crime-fiction writer. And this is my first visit to a police station.

Dinkar: 'Excuse me, Sir, I have a report to file.'

The man sitting on the other side was a sub-inspector. His nameplate read Virendra Kaushal. He was a middle-aged man who looked sensible—a rare quality for a policeman.

Virendra: 'What happened?'

Dinkar: 'I lost my handbag at the bus stop this afternoon. I had just got off the bus when a guy snatched it from my hands. I tried to run after him, but he was too fast.'

Virendra: 'Okay, can you describe the guy?'

Dinkar: 'Well, I didn't get a chance to have a good look at his face, but he was a lean man, about 5'9" or 5'10".'

Virendra: 'Anything else about his appearance that can be of help?'

Dinkar: 'He was wearing blue jeans and a half-sleeve T-shirt. The colour was something between red and orange. I'm afraid that's all I noticed.'

Virendra gave me a casual look before saying, 'I'm afraid this description alone can't help us much. Half the college-going crowd would match it. Crime is on the rise in this area; a lot of unknown faces are operating these days. We will surely try to catch the bastard. Anyway, what was in the handbag?'

Dinkar became a bit nervous before replying, 'Sir, the bag had a handwritten rough draft of a novel that I'm currently writing. It may not seem valuable to you, but it's the only copy I had.'

Virendra's face went through a series of expressions before he finally said, 'Well, was the story interesting?'

Dinkar smiled for the first time and said, 'I seriously hope so. I went to a publishing agency to show them the rough draft, but they were busy today. So, when I was returning from their office, this incident happened.'

Virendra: 'What kind of story was it anyway?'

Dinkar: 'The story of an ordinary thug who tries to become the most powerful criminal in the city.'

Virendra, now looking quite interested: 'Really? Well, does he succeed?'

Dinkar: 'Well, you'll need to read the story for that.'

Virendra: 'So why don't you tell me the story yourself? I wouldn't mind listening.'

Dinkar remained undecided for some time but then realised he had nothing better to do anyway. So he began the story: 'Okay, so the story starts when…'

(ii)

At the same time that Dinkar was narrating his story to Virendra Kaushal, someone else was reading it. His name was Jaggi. He was 5'10" and was wearing blue jeans and a half-sleeve T-shirt whose colour was something between red and orange.

A man entered the room in which Jaggi was sitting. His name was Govind, a longtime friend of Jaggi and his partner in crime.

Govind: 'I don't know what you've been reading for the last two hours.'

Jaggi: 'It was the only thing I got out of the bag I snatched today.'

Govind: 'Throw that crap out of the window and do some real work. Our business doesn't allow time for pursuing literature.'

Jaggi: 'It's not literature, my friend—it's a guidebook.'

Govind: 'I don't get it. What's in this book?'

Jaggi: 'It's about a small-time con like me, who starts progressing at an *inorganic* speed.'

Govind: 'Inorganic? What kind of shit are you talking about? I still don't understand.'

Jaggi: 'Leave your ignorance aside for a moment and just tell me—where can I get a revolver?'

(iii)

The protagonist of the book gets frustrated with his low life as a street thug and starts dreaming of making a big name in the world of crime. His first step toward his goal is to make sure he has all the groundwork in place before he begins. He prepares his team as well as all the ammunition needed for his future endeavours.

Jaggi's plan wasn't much different from the book. In the next few days, Jaggi not only got hold of a revolver but also recruited a gang of trusted allies. Apart from him and Govind, two more people joined—Madan and Hemant.

As a small-time criminal, you can snatch a bag, a gold chain, or maybe overpower an isolated man and take away his belongings, but you can never make much out of these acts. What you need is planning, timely execution, and the right target. But without a team and weapons, it's quite difficult to do so.

A revolver reduces your chances of being caught manifold. Not only can you scare the life out of people just by showing it—you rarely need to pull the trigger. You can rob a lot of people in short intervals without harming them. A revolver costs a lot, but it's a good investment.

All that is needed is to isolate the victims—rich-looking old people, couples who are afraid their secret meetings will be exposed, or anyone from whom money can be extracted. Just don't get too greedy. Lie low after every strike, and make sure people are scared enough to give you their money but never hurt, so the police don't start taking you very seriously.

If all this had been done by any other gang, they would be partying hard every night. But this was just the primary phase of what Jaggi wanted to achieve—a very high rank in the crime world. Power never comes easy; it is built step by step. And that was exactly the plan. In a short span of time, Jaggi was able to collect enough money for his next step. Now he had weapons for all his colleagues, a rented one-room hideout on the far edge of the city as an emergency facility, and a lot of courage.

The next stage was to rob a jeweller's shop. A bold step by any measure—but a risk worth taking. With four armed men and a carefully executed plan, it was not difficult to rob a shop. Choose a shop with a single doorkeeper-cum-guard and minimum staff, and if the shop is located slightly off the main road, your chances of success increase manifold. All that is needed is proper timing—strike when the number of customers is the lowest. Three men should enter, take everyone at gunpoint, and collect as much cash and gold as possible. Generally, jewellery shops are insured, so nobody tries to act like a hero.

But the real talent lies in *not getting caught* after a successful robbery. All the criminals of an area are known to the police, so the police will be on your tail as soon as they get a clue about your face. Wearing a false moustache and beard is never a bad idea. Wearing a locket of any other religion and prominently showing it to the people in the shop further helps in confusing the investigation. Before leaving the shop premises, make sure all mobile and landline phones are taken care of, and close the shutter of the shop both when you enter and when you exit, so nobody outside can immediately alert the authorities.

Most unsuccessful robbers go wrong while trying to run away from the city as soon as possible. This usually becomes a flawed strategy—they are often caught at toll booths, or at least leave traces that the police later follow. Even their sudden absence from the city becomes suspicious. The best way is *not* to run—behave as naturally as possible, sit on all the stolen material, and not spend it. Don't even contact a fence (a man who deals in purchasing and selling stolen items) beforehand. Let the dust settle, and make your move when the right time comes.

Jaggi did all of it successfully—but what followed was unexpected!

(iv)

Dinkar was getting ready to go to sleep when the doorbell rang. It was Jaggi.

Dinkar: 'Who are you?'

Jaggi: 'My name is Jaggi. You don't know me, but I know you very well. I got your address from this bag.'

Jaggi was holding the same bag that he had stolen from Dinkar, and it didn't take long for Dinkar to realise that the man standing in front of him was the thief himself.

Dinkar: 'You bastard... you thief! You took away my hard work of the last six months. Let me just call the police!'

Jaggi: 'Please... just listen to me. Give me two minutes. Let me explain.'

Dinkar stopped. Looking at Jaggi's face, he hesitated before saying, 'Sub-Inspector Virendra Kaushal called me this evening. He said a lot of action is taking place in the city exactly as described in the book. He feels someone is using the book to actually commit crimes. Is that true? Are you really doing all the things as per the book? Is it really working?'

The last question gave away Dinkar's curiosity—the excitement that his words could actually be turned into real action.

Even Jaggi sensed it. He said slowly, 'Yes. What you wrote worked for me. Everything you wrote was actionable. I made a lot of money using it. I even robbed a jeweller's shop today—very successfully. But now I have two problems.'

Dinkar: 'And they are?'

Jaggi: 'The shop I looted belongs to Raghav Singh, a very big name in the underworld. The jewellery shop was just a front for converting his black money into white. I didn't know the shop belonged to him, but I found out later. For now, he doesn't know it was me and my gang, but soon enough he will. And then he will hunt me down and kill me with his own hands. I don't want to die.'

Dinkar: 'And what exactly is the second problem?'

Jaggi: 'I don't have the final chapter of the book. I thought I wouldn't need it—I believed I'd have enough money after the loot and could settle down somewhere. But Raghav Singh won't let me live after what I did to him. Please tell me what the last chapter of the book is. How does the story end?'

A faint smile appeared on Dinkar's face before he said, 'Actually, I'm yet to write the final chapter. But I have already made up my mind about the climax. The main character of the book—the thief—gets killed in the last chapter.'

What followed was silence.

(v)

Jaggi: 'What do you mean?'

Dinkar: 'Are you deaf or what? The thief gets killed in the end. You know—crime never pays. A criminal is supposed to pay for what he's done.'

Jaggi: 'Oh my God...'

Dinkar: 'You look unhappy.'

Jaggi: 'I've just been killed literally. I *deserve* to be pissed.'

Dinkar: 'Well, in my defence, I never invited you to play the lead role. Anyway, what else did you expect?'

Jaggi: 'I expected some imagination! All you writers are alike—you can't think of anything new. What's so wonderful about your story? A guy becomes a big criminal and dies in the end—what an original idea! You know something? When I didn't know the ending, I always thought the story would end differently. But you're just like the other jerks. I'm actually disappointed in you.'

Dinkar had never thought he would be on the receiving end. He was being lectured—logically—by a petty criminal. And Jaggi had a point. Maybe the story *did* need a different ending.

Then Dinkar said to Jaggi, 'So you want me to write a different end to this story… and you think that by saving the thief in my story, you can actually get out of trouble?'

Jaggi: 'Yes. I sincerely believe that. Whatever you wrote, I tried in real life—and things happened exactly as you predicted. Except, of course, the last incident… when I accidentally robbed the wrong shop.'

Dinkar: 'Okay, Jaggi. I'll write something else—but not to help you continue your illegal activities. You have to promise me you'll stop all of this. And you're going to do everything I tell you to.'

Jaggi: 'I agree. Just save my life.'

Dinkar: 'This is going to be interesting—a story that will bring down a bigger criminal instead of a small crook.'

Jaggi was horrified as he understood the meaning of this statement.

(vi)

Virendra Kaushal got a call from Dinkar Joshi asking for an urgent meeting.

Dinkar: 'Well... how should I put it? I need your help in understanding something. Could you help me?'

Virendra: 'Sure. What do you want to know?'

Dinkar: 'Tell me everything you know about Raghav Singh.'

Virendra took his time before replying, as if he was arranging the information in his head so that it would be precise yet effective.

Virendra: 'How should I put it... He's a man desperately trying to become the godfather of this town. He's involved in a variety of criminal activities, runs legitimate businesses to cover his illegal income, and has strong connections in the police as well as in politics. In all, he's dangerous enough for one to not go around inquiring about him.'

He paused to take a breath. Then his expression suddenly changed, as if a set of mental calculations had fallen into place.

Virendra: 'Recently, one of his jewellery shops got robbed... and interestingly, the modus operandi was the same as in your book.'

(Then, with a sudden increase in tone)

'What are you not telling me, Dinkar?'

Ignoring the question, Dinkar continued: 'If you know this man is so dangerous, why haven't you or your department done something about him?'

Virendra: 'Nobody wants to take the initiative. It means that even though not all policemen are in his pocket, still nobody wants to take the chance of fighting such a powerful enemy. It means, "Why bother? If the next policeman isn't concerned, why should I be?" It means nobody wants to start something he will regret tomorrow.'

Dinkar: 'But you wouldn't mind if someone else makes a different move?'

Virendra asked suspiciously: 'What do you want to do?'

Dinkar: 'I just want to change the climax of my story.'

(vii)

Dinkar took his time before he called Jaggi to his house.

Dinkar: 'I have given it a lot of thought. You have two options. First, you run—as fast as you can.'

Jaggi: 'I don't need a writer to come up with *that* solution. Even I thought about it. But the day Raghav Singh finds out that I've crossed him, he'll hunt me down and kill me himself.'

Dinkar: 'Really?'

Jaggi: 'Yes. He's done it before. He's too dangerous.'

Dinkar: 'So that brings us to the second option—very ambitious, very dramatic, and the chances of failure are high.'

Jaggi: 'I've run out of choices. I'm ready to take the odds.'

Dinkar: 'Alright. First of all, we need a new recruit on your team.'

Dinkar had taken full advantage of his association with Virendra Kaushal. By now, he knew all the dynamics of the city's underbelly. As with any other industry, crime too had fierce competition—*cut-throat,* quite literally. Raghav Singh's biggest rival was Nisar Pathan, and he was going to be at the epicentre of the first strike against Raghav Singh.

Jaggi: 'A new recruit for what?'

Dinkar: 'To rob another jewellery store. It's also owned by Raghav Singh.'

Jaggi: 'You crazy, lunatic bastard! I didn't come here to get myself killed.'

Dinkar: 'I know. Just listen. First, find a new guy for your team. Don't let him realise he's working for you. Don't give him your real names either. All he needs to know is that your entire team works for Nisar Pathan.'

Jaggi stared at Dinkar in disbelief, slowly beginning to understand the plan.

Dinkar continued: 'You, your gang, and the new guy will rob the shop. Then everyone will assume that if this shop was robbed by Nisar Pathan, the previous one must have been his handiwork too.'

Jaggi: 'But how will everyone know that? Will we wait for this guy to announce Pathan's involvement on a loudspeaker?'

Dinkar: 'Oh, did I forget to mention? After you successfully pull off the robbery, remember to shoot him in the leg.'

Jaggi: 'Then he'll think Pathan betrayed him. Fantastic!'

Dinkar: 'And what's the American expression for that? He'll "sing like a bird" in front of the police.'

(viii)

The plan was executed flawlessly by Jaggi and his team. The fall guy did exactly what was expected of him—he pointed his finger at Nisar Pathan. He couldn't give much description of Jaggi and his associates, as they had taken precautions: wearing false beards and moustaches, and keeping their eyes hidden behind sunglasses. However, with the big fish—Pathan—now in sight, the police were far more concerned about playing their cards right so that the city's power balance wouldn't be disturbed.

Just as with Raghav Singh, the police were not comfortable grabbing Pathan by the collar, knowing there would be repercussions. But that didn't seem to bother Raghav Singh. He initiated a full-blown attack on Pathan's establishments. Initially, Pathan was too busy defending his property and people to sort out his issues with Raghav Singh. And once he gained some footing, he was too furious to call for peace. As expected, he retaliated with full force. After being hit by two consecutive robberies at his jewellery shops, Raghav Singh was now bleeding further from Pathan's direct assault.

Dinkar's first strike had achieved exactly what had once seemed overly ambitious and dramatic.

Jaggi was at Dinkar's house, assessing the damage they had dealt to Raghav Singh.

Jaggi: 'You played beautifully. We're out of the soup now. Really, thank you.'

Dinkar gave him a disapproving look before speaking. 'You're mistaken. Although we seem to have crippled him, this isn't over. He has lost some of his physical and economic strength because of the conflict with Pathan, but he isn't finished. He still has support from powerful people. And you can't ignore the possibility of him finding out that *we* are the ones orchestrating this war against him. He still has enough power to crush us under his boot. We need a second strike—fast—before he regroups.'

Jaggi sighed. 'I assume you already have another plan ready.'

Dinkar smiled and said: 'Absolutely.'

Jaggi: 'You're enjoying this, aren't you?'

Dinkar: 'As I said before—absolutely.'

The meeting that followed included all the members of Jaggi's team.

Govind: 'So what do you want to do this time?'

Dinkar: 'Kidnap small children.'

Jaggi: 'Hey, what are you talking about? What children? I don't even know if Raghav Singh or Pathan have kids young enough to kidnap. And even if they do, that would be the most dangerous move—we can't handle the kind of security they'd have.'

Govind: 'Yes, and it's extremely dangerous. What do you think—kidnapping is easy? Leaving aside a few isolated cases, kidnappers are *always* caught. And kidnapping small children—oh my god! The public, the police, everyone goes mad. Once they get a scent of the kidnappers, they want to tear them apart like cannibals. Child kidnappers are the most hated criminals in society.'

Jaggi: 'And they climb to the top of the most-wanted list in hours. Catching them becomes the police's top priority—after terrorists.'

Dinkar: 'In that case, I think I've made my point.'

Nobody understood the remark. Everyone stared at Dinkar, waiting for an explanation.

Dinkar: 'First things first—yes, I want to kidnap small children, and it won't be difficult, because I don't want to kidnap anybody remotely related to Pathan or Raghav Singh. On the contrary, I want to kidnap children whose families can't even afford breakfast, let alone security. I want you to kidnap four to five small children from the slums.'

Jaggi: 'But why? How would that help us?'

Dinkar: 'Do exactly as I say. Just make sure the children are taken care of properly.'

(ix)

By that night, Jaggi and his gang had gathered the required number of children.

Jaggi: 'Now what?'

Dinkar: 'Raghav Singh has a chemical factory on the outskirts of the city. It has a big compound and a lot of isolated space. I want you to place the children inside that compound. You should be able to find some unused cottage, room, or storage area—leave the children inside any such place.'

Govind: 'And then what?'

Dinkar: 'I asked you to keep an eye on the police station, so that if the parents of those children went there, we'd know. What's the status?'

Govind: 'One of our guys was there. He confirmed that the parents went to the police station to complain about their missing children, but the police sent them back. They didn't take the matter seriously.'

Dinkar: 'Wonderful.'

All the children were taken to the factory compound. There was security, but not enough to detect what Jaggi and his men were doing. Fortunately, they found a half-filled warehouse where they left the sedated children.

Dinkar: 'Now we need to make anonymous phone calls to some newspapers and the police department, telling them that the kidnapped children are being held inside Raghav Singh's factory.'

Jaggi: 'Oh, you're such an idiot. Who would believe that Raghav Singh kidnapped these children? What ransom could he possibly get from their parents? As Govind said earlier, even the police aren't taking the matter seriously. All this drama for such a lame trick?'

Dinkar: 'Did I forget to mention? The calls we make won't just give the location of the children—they'll also give the *motive* for the kidnapping. We'll tell them that Raghav Singh is using his so-called chemical factory as a front for kidnapping slum children and harvesting their organs to sell in Africa and Arab countries.'

Jaggi: 'My God... that will create chaos in the city. People will become bloodthirsty for Raghav Singh.'

Dinkar: 'Yes, my friend. If people hate child kidnappers, imagine what they'll do to someone accused of selling their organs.'

Govind: 'But we won't have any proof to back up this story. I don't even know whether these children have organs worth transplanting.'

Dinkar: 'The beauty is—we don't need to prove anything. Once the news spreads, nobody will even bother looking for facts. There will be mobs on the streets demanding Raghav Singh's head.'

Jaggi: 'And what do we gain from this elaborate plan?'

Dinkar: 'We kick away his internal support from the police and politicians. Nobody in their right mind would want to be associated with him after this scandal. And as someone once told me—once I break the status quo, there will be plenty of people in the police department who won't mind going after Raghav Singh.'

(x)

This was the second success in a row for Dinkar, as everything unfolded exactly the way he had predicted. After the press received the anonymous tip about slum children who were supposedly going to lose their precious organs so they could be sold in foreign countries, they went into action. The media created enormous pressure on the police to accompany them and search the factory premises. And as soon as the children were found, all hell broke loose. Raghav Singh was arrested within an hour. Many of his known associates went underground, and suddenly all the powerful people who once supported him stopped taking his calls.

The next day, when Jaggi and his gang entered Dinkar's house, they found him in a grim mood, reading the newspaper.

Jaggi: 'Why do you look depressed?'

Dinkar: 'Raghav Singh's lawyers have got him out of police custody on bail. The case will begin soon, but until then he'll be out in the open.'

Jaggi: 'What are you implying?'

Dinkar: 'That the danger is still there. We've weakened him, no doubt, but he hasn't become a beggar on the streets. Even in his reduced state, he can still crush us. You hear me—*us,* not just you.'

Jaggi: 'Why are you panicking? You must have a third act, some conclusive strike against him?'

Dinkar: 'I'm afraid not. I can't think of anything imaginative that could help us. A sort of writer's block—you wouldn't understand. Anyway, I think I need to come up with an exit strategy.'

Jaggi: 'Exit strategy? What do you mean? Oh my God... you're saying we're *still* not out of the woods?'

Govind: 'And we've messed things up even more by asking for your help than we ever did on our own. Raghav Singh won't leave us now.'

Jaggi: 'He'll kill me with his bare hands. I need to leave this city as soon as possible.'

Jaggi didn't wait for Dinkar to respond. He simply turned and walked out of the house.

(xi)

It was late at night when Raghav Singh received a call on his home landline.

Raghav Singh: 'Who's calling?'

Caller: 'That's not important. The question is—are you interested in knowing who has been screwing you at regular intervals?'

Raghav Singh: 'The whole city knows that. Pathan did this, and I swear to God I will take vengeance.'

Caller: 'Well, what if I tell you that all this is a big scam? The real player is someone else, and he used Pathan's name as a cover.'

Raghav Singh had never considered this possibility. What if there really was someone else? Pathan wasn't foolish enough to start such an open war without a clear motive.

Raghav Singh: 'Why should I believe you?'

The caller went on to describe everything that had happened since a small-time thief accidentally robbed a jewellery shop he should never have touched, and all the desperate damage control he had done to save himself.

By this time, Raghav Singh was convinced that someone had indeed played a grand game with him.

Raghav Singh: 'Fine. Tell me the name of the son of a bitch.'

Caller: 'How does ten lakh sound as the fee for this service?'

Raghav Singh: 'Done.'

Caller: 'Come to Central Market and look inside the big dumpster. Leave the money there, and you will find what you're looking for in a small plastic pouch.'

Raghav Singh personally went to the Central Market with a party of four armed men. He found the plastic pouch inside the dumpster and left the money as instructed. The paper inside the pouch contained the name and current location of Jaggi.

(xii)

Unaware of the betrayal, Jaggi was sleeping in the one-room hideout he had arranged for emergencies. He woke up suddenly when he first heard the screeching of tyres, followed by the sound of his front door being smashed open. The beast known as Raghav Singh was inside his safe house—with a revolver in his hand and hatred in his eyes. Without any dramatic dialogues usually associated with such scenes in Indian movies, Raghav simply pulled the trigger.

Jaggi felt a warm sensation in his chest, as if someone had stabbed a burning knife near his heart. All he could think in that moment was that the story had reached its predictable end.

But that was not the case.

The moment the first shot was fired, half a dozen policemen stormed into the room with their weapons drawn.

More would have entered, but there was barely any space. The entire crew, including Raghav Singh, was arrested by Sub-Inspector Virendra Kaushal. Jaggi was immediately taken to a nearby hospital, where after surgery he was declared out of danger.

(xiii)

The next morning, Jaggi had an early visitor.

Dinkar: 'So, how are you feeling?'

Jaggi: 'Alive!'

Dinkar: 'Great. Good to know that a bullet hasn't cost you your sense of humour.'

Jaggi: 'Well, the bullet was more interested in my heart. Now can somebody explain to me what just happened?'

Dinkar: 'Certainly. As you know, I had run out of ideas. I knew the child-kidnapping case wouldn't survive against Raghav Singh in court. He was like chewing gum stuck in our hair—we needed solid proof. So I gambled with an idea. I called him and told him I could give him your location if he paid me ten lakh rupees. When he took the bait and came to kill you, we caught him in the act.'

Jaggi couldn't believe what he had just heard. He started screaming and cursing at the top of his voice. Dinkar had expected this and remained quiet until Jaggi finally calmed down a little.

Jaggi: 'Why did you do that? You knew it was dangerous. I asked you to help me save my life, and you offered it on a platter!'

Dinkar: 'You need to understand—by involving me, it wasn't just *your* life that was in danger. Mine was in the crossfire too. I had to protect myself.'

Jaggi: 'But he could have killed me! He *did* shoot me, for God's sake. I survived by luck. If that bullet had actually hit my heart, I would've been dead! Then what?'

Dinkar: 'Frankly, Jaggi... we would still have caught Raghav Singh. Only it would've been for murder instead of attempted murder.'

Jaggi: 'Oh my God. You've turned into a cold-blooded monster—putting yourself ahead of everyone else.'

Dinkar: 'This coming from a man who steals and robs innocent people for a living? And don't forget—it was *you* who stole my story, you who wanted to become the most powerful man in the city, you who messed up and came begging for my help. And yes, I *did* save your life in the end. I took risks because I had to. But you survived, so be grateful for that.'

It took Jaggi nearly an hour to let go of his anger—reluctantly, because after all, he had survived.

Jaggi sighed: 'Alright, let bygones be bygones. Now what are you going to do?'

Dinkar: 'Well, thanks to you, the first thing I'm going to do is change the climax of my story. And what about you? What are you planning?'

Jaggi: 'Let's just say... I'm going to wait for your next novel.'

3

THE HAPPINESS OF OTHERS

Party Night

Has anyone ever wondered why everybody's closets are filled with so many clothes? Sure, everyone likes to have choices—but clearly, we don't wear most of our clothes. All the clothes we bought were loved at the time of purchase; now, however, not so much! Doesn't it give a rare glimpse into human behaviour? We like a lot of things at first, but after a time, they feel like a burden.

Jai Handa was in a similar dilemma right now—what to pick for the office party? Office parties were otherwise an ordinary affair for him, but today was different. Today, he was going to introduce everybody to Mitali Sharma, especially to his boss Harvinder Singh and his wife.

Jai was a marginally handsome man in his early 30s, working at an advertising agency owned by Harvinder Singh. Jai hated Harvinder from his gut but never had the conviction to confront him. Today, however, was different. He glanced at the off-white envelope lying on his desk and said to himself once again, *'Yes, today it's going to be different.'*

About One Month Ago

Jai came out of Harvinder's cabin with the look of a dog that had been kicked in the stomach. Humiliation was written all over his face, with a strict warning beneath—*don't talk to me about what happened in the cabin.*

A couple of hours later, during lunch, Aniruddh Mathur, his only friend in the office, approached him.

Aniruddh (looking at his grim expression): 'That bad, huh?'

Jai: 'My self-respect hits a new low every time I exit his cabin. There seems to be no end to my humiliation. If he thinks I'm so bad at my job, why does he even bother keeping me? He should just fire me.'

Aniruddh: 'Come on, buddy, don't say that. The fact that you're still here means you're important to the company. Don't lose heart—your day will come.'

Aniruddh never knew his prophecy would come true in less than a week.

It was a Sunday afternoon when Jai heard some noises coming from his adjacent flat. The apartment had a new tenant—a single, beautiful girl—and Jai had been wondering whether to approach her. But today, it sounded like she had a visitor, *possibly a boyfriend*. Jai felt his curiosity rising. The voices died down, and at that moment, Jai went to the door-eye to see who was leaving.

The man walking out, trying to be inconspicuous, was in his mid-40s. Jai recognised him instantly—it was Harvinder Singh.

The next few days were difficult for Jai. He understood Harvinder was having an affair with the girl next door, but he didn't know what to do with this information. After three days of non-stop thinking, Jai reluctantly approached her.

Jai: 'Hi, I'm your neighbour, Jai Handa.'

Girl: 'Pleased to make your acquaintance, Jai. I'm Mitali Sharma.'

Jai befriended Mitali with little effort. In the two weeks since he first saw Harvinder at Mitali's apartment, he had witnessed a couple more visits. Still, he was unclear about what to do. It was again Aniruddh who gave him a breakthrough when he told Jai about a job opening at another advertising firm.

It was only a matter of time before Jai appeared for an interview and got a job confirmation letter—inside that off-white envelope. He was now ready with what he wanted to do with the information, and he chose the upcoming office party to make his move.

He was going to destroy Harvinder Singh.

Party Day

Though it took some convincing, Jai was able to get Mitali to attend the party with him. He hadn't told her the name of the firm he worked for, just to be safe.

Jai and Mitali entered the party floor together. Everyone seemed busy with conversations and booze. Jai anxiously scanned the room for Mr and Mrs Harvinder Singh. He was a little scared—what if Mrs Singh wasn't present? His whole plan would fall apart.

But for once, fate favoured him. He spotted the couple engaged in conversation. Jai approached them, holding Mitali by the arm, while she was casually sipping her drink. No one realised what was happening until Jai was standing right before them. Suddenly, eyes turned, and the colour drained from the faces of Harvinder and Mitali. Mrs Singh stood there with a bemused expression.

Jai finally said, 'Mrs Singh, let me introduce you to your husband's girlfriend.'

And all hell broke loose.

Harvinder's first reaction was to deny knowing the girl—an amateur move if you ask me, because it infuriated Mitali beyond measure. Her next sentence was a bombshell.

Mitali: 'What the hell do you mean you don't know me? I'm pregnant with your child, and you say you don't know me? I'll kill you, bastard!'

Jai was too euphoric to pay attention to what followed, but witnesses swear it was one hell of a show.

A lot happened in the next week. Before anyone could fire him, Jai resigned. He also received a court notice to appear in the divorce case filed by Mrs Singh.

One and a Half Years Later

Jai had settled quite well in his new job. His current employer, L. Subramaniyam, was a decent fellow. Jai was not humiliated by him—and that was the biggest perk of the job.

He had just finished his day's work and was about to leave when he received an unexpected call from his former employer.

Harvinder: 'Jai, can you drive by my office today on your way home?'

Confused, Jai said yes.

There was nobody in the office when he arrived. The thought that Harvinder might have plotted something sinister began to unsettle him—*perhaps a gun? A knife? A heavy metal flower pot?* Jai felt a shiver run down his spine and chided himself for not informing anyone about this visit.

To his surprise, when he entered the cabin, Harvinder appeared to be in a pleasant mood, holding a glass of his favourite scotch and leaning back in his executive chair. As soon as he saw Jai, he offered him a seat and a drink. Jai, still uneasy, accepted.

Harvinder: 'Today, the divorce court ruled in my favour. My wife's request was denied.'

Jai was stunned. Everything in the case had gone against Harvinder. The court should have ruled in his wife's favour on grounds of adultery. But we all know how the system works—Singh must have greased many palms.

Harvinder, however, understood what Jai was thinking.

Harvinder: 'No, Jai. I didn't bribe my way out. I won the trial because my wife couldn't prove I was having an affair.'

Jai: 'What are you talking about? Your girlfriend was carrying your baby!'

Harvinder (laughing): 'No, she wasn't. That's exactly what she said in court. After medical examination, the doctor declared she had never been pregnant in her life. Come to think of it—she wasn't even my girlfriend.'

Jai: 'What are you talking about? I don't understand!'

Harvinder: 'I know. Let me explain. I at least owe you that—that's why I called you here today.' (He paused to gather his thoughts.) 'I married my wife smitten by her beauty. She married me for my money. I was okay with it until I realised she was... well, a bitch.'

'She wasn't happy being the wife of a rich man; she wanted to be rich and independent herself. The easiest way was to divorce her wealthy husband and get a big settlement. So, she hired a private detective agency to watch me—not because she suspected anything, but because she wanted dirt on me.'

'When I realised I was being followed, I became cautious. Now, you know me—I had a few indiscretions here and there, but I was never in a serious affair. Still, if she caught me even once, I'd be done.'

'By then I, too, wanted to get rid of her. So, I created the opportunity myself. I arranged for a girl to live next to your apartment and started visiting her. Eventually, you spotted me. But you didn't act immediately—I knew you hated me enough to use it against me but not at the cost of your job. So, I arranged the job for you at Subramaniyam's firm.'

Jai: 'What? So, Aniruddh...?'

Harvinder: 'Yes. He was my inside man. He led you to the bait—and you took it. That was all I needed for you to drop the bomb on my wife. She took the bait too and filed for divorce. But in court, Mitali refused to recognise me, let alone claim she was pregnant. As far as you were concerned—everyone knew you hated me. You could have mistaken the identity of the man visiting your neighbour. The hallway is dimly lit anyway.'

Jai: 'But what was the purpose of all this drama? If you didn't want to divorce your wife, what was the point?'

Harvinder: 'The point is—there's a difference between *my wife divorcing me* and *me divorcing my wife*. If she divorces me, I have to give her a large settlement. But if *I* divorce *her*, she gets nothing. She needed a reason to divorce me, and I needed one too. Now that it's established that she brought false charges against me—I have valid grounds to divorce her. All thanks to you.'

Jai couldn't bear it any more. He began walking towards the door.

Harvinder called out, 'You know what? Aniruddh was right about one thing. I didn't fire you long ago because you were important to me. Where else would I have found an idiot like you?'

4

EVERYBODY KNOWS IT

DSP Jayant Sinha's House

Jayant Sinha was having one of those days when there are simply no good options—only bad or miserable ones. And, frankly, he'd been having these kinds of days rather frequently ever since he met Aditya Thakur. Thakur was the kind of junior dreaded by every man in his line of work. He was fearless, adamant, and overly aggressive, but his biggest disqualification was that he didn't give a hoot about how the system worked—and that pissed off everybody from top to bottom.

Jayant Sinha, a veteran in the force, had outlasted many honest cops in his long career, and at times even relied on them to run interference for his schemes. But those officers, though honest, were afraid—afraid of consequences. They wanted to preserve their sense of principle without rocking the boat. They just wanted to be left alone. Insubordination was never a trait he found in them—which, incidentally, was the middle name of Aditya Thakur, a young man with a lot to prove.

It was 11:00 pm when Jayant took his third peg. He was in his mid-fifties, a well-built man with a dense moustache and very liberal views on integrity and flexible loyalty. That's why he always played for the winning side and was handsomely rewarded for it. At the moment, he was being paid four times his salary by Bhushan Bhai—the biggest gangster in the city.

Earlier that day, Aditya had raided an illegal godown belonging to Bhushan Bhai and confiscated everything inside it. It was Jayant's duty to ensure such raids never happened—or at least warn Bhushan Bhai if such an action was inevitable. Jayant had failed on both counts: Aditya never bothered informing his immediate superior (Jayant) about the raid, and now Jayant would have to face Bhushan Bhai the next morning to explain. *It's going to get ugly,* thought Jayant, finishing his drink.

Bhushan Bhai's Bungalow, Next Morning

Keshav Tripathi was a tall, lean man with cruel eyes and even crueller intentions. He glared at Jayant and spat, 'Why the hell do we pay you so much money, thinking you're a senior officer, when in reality, you're not even as useful as a constable?'

Jayant could feel the blood rush to his ears in anger, but Keshav Tripathi—the right-hand man of Bhushan Bhai—was not known for mercy. Jayant kept his composure and stayed silent.

Bhushan Bhai sat on his trademark single sofa, smoking his favourite cigar, deep in thought. He hadn't said a single word since Jayant entered the room. Once Keshav was done thrashing Jayant verbally, everyone looked towards Bhushan for further instructions.

He was known in the criminal circles as a man who rarely lost his cool, but no one mistook his calm for weakness—those who did never lived long enough to correct the mistake. He finally spoke in a very low voice:

'This should never happen again.'

That one sentence sent a chilling shiver down Jayant's spine.

Police Headquarters, That Afternoon

The first thing Jayant did upon entering his chamber was call Aditya, who arrived within minutes. Jayant didn't offer him a seat, and Aditya didn't expect to be extended that courtesy.

Jayant stared at him for a few moments—wondering if this man would even survive the month—before he barked, 'What you did yesterday undermined my authority. You're supposed to inform me and get my consent before taking any action like conducting a raid. The procedure exists for a reason—you know that.'

Aditya had expected this confrontation and wasn't shaken by his senior's annoyance—in fact, he seemed to be enjoying it a little. He kept his tone calm as he replied, 'Sir, time was of the essence yesterday. They could have moved the material if I hadn't reacted quickly.'

Jayant knew it was rubbish. The reality was that Aditya didn't trust him—and with good reason. Everybody knew Jayant was the inside man for Bhushan Bhai.

'Don't give me that bullshit,' Jayant snapped. 'From now on, I want advance notice of *any* action you take—whether against a pickpocket or a gangster. If you defy me again, God knows it'll be your last time. Am I clear?'

'Of course,' Aditya replied coolly. He didn't feel the need to elaborate and walked out, not allowing Jayant a chance to continue the conversation.

'Bloody arrogant bastard,' Jayant muttered.

One Week Later

A week passed without incident, but the calm was broken when Aditya entered Jayant's office with Shantilal Shah.

Shantilal was an old-school policeman on the brink of retirement—shrewd and well-connected. Though he'd been in the department much longer than Jayant, his position was still junior to Aditya's, which said a lot about Aditya's efficiency and ambition. Shantilal knew the ins and outs of the criminal world and the police department, making him occasionally useful.

Aditya said, 'Sir, I'm leading a raid at another warehouse in the outer city area. I have information about a major narcotics shipment there.' As soon as he mentioned the location, both Jayant and Shantilal realised who owned it—Abdul Lala.

Lala had risen in the crime world with brute force. A hothead and borderline psychotic, he ranked just below Bhushan Bhai. But neither Jayant nor Shantilal mentioned this to Aditya.

Jayant granted permission for the raid. However, by the time the police reached the location, the warehouse was empty. Someone had leaked the information to Lala.

Aditya remained in a foul mood for the rest of the week. His colleagues wisely avoided him. Assuming the warehouse belonged to Bhushan Bhai, he didn't bother to verify it. Everyone thought Aditya was preparing his next strike against Bhushan, and the atmosphere remained tense.

With no major action possible, Aditya began targeting Bhushan's low-level associates. Some were arrested, threatened, and beaten.

An enraged Keshav Tripathi called Jayant: 'If you can't keep your dog on a leash, let me do it for you. Arrange a meeting with that bastard.'

Jayant managed a rare smile. *This will be interesting,* he thought.

At the Party

Jayant invited Aditya to a party hosted by a prominent industrialist. Aditya was reluctant at first but eventually agreed—a change of environment wouldn't hurt.

Upon reaching the venue, Jayant excused himself, pretending to meet an old friend, and asked Aditya to enjoy himself. It wasn't long before Tripathi approached Aditya.

Tripathi: 'Do you know me?'

Aditya: 'Only by reputation—and the photo in my case file.'

Tripathi: 'Then you know I don't give a damn about body count. People fear me—and for good reason. Policemen come and go—we stay. We have a system, an understanding. But you? You're a problem. You're jamming the machinery, and I don't like it. Get on board, or the alternative is not pretty.'

Tripathi watched Aditya's face for a reaction. There was none.

Aditya: 'You're scum. Your boss is scum. And so is

every filth that thinks it can rule this city. You say you scare people, yet it's *you* who came to *me* tonight. I don't play by rules. You give me options—but I won't give you any. Your fate is sealed. I will break you. And when time comes, you'll wish you'd never crossed my path. You play dirty. Well, Tripathi, *I play ugly*. You'll find out soon enough.'

Aditya walked away, leaving a stunned crowd witnessing the clash between the arrogance of crime and the defiance of law.

Next Evening

Keshav Tripathi's body was found near the docks.

Jayant couldn't sleep that night.

Next Day

Jayant personally took over the investigation—it also gave him an excuse to delay meeting Bhushan. He was sweating constantly, dreading the consequences, and fervently cursing Aditya for his recklessness.

There wasn't a shred of evidence linking Aditya. The bullet didn't match his service gun—it came from a foreign-made pistol, illegal and nearly impossible to acquire on the black market. No such weapon was logged in the police evidence room either.

Shantilal Shah swore Aditya had been with him the whole time on the other side of the city. Shantilal wasn't above giving false testimony if incentivised—so maybe someone else was involved. *Maybe Lala… someone who wanted to displace Bhushan,* thought Jayant. He was never sure.

Tripathi's murder was ruled a professional hit. Jayant had

never seen Bhushan so furious. Still, Aditya was questioned and acquitted.

Days Later

Aditya walked into Jayant's room.

Aditya: 'Sir, I need your permission for a raid.'

Jayant: 'Who now? Another godown of Bhushan Bhai? Or someone else who insulted you needs to be removed?'

Ignoring the sarcasm, Aditya continued, 'Nothing to do with Bhushan. It's about another gangster—Abdul Lala. While looking for evidence against Bhushan, I stumbled onto low-ranking members of Lala's gang. They've agreed to become state witnesses.'

Jayant (tense): 'Did you apply third degree on them?'

Aditya: 'That's not important. What's important is I have incriminating evidence against Lala and I'm going to raid his house. You asked me to keep you in the loop—and here I am. If you'll hurry up, I have a criminal to catch.'

Jayant was compelled to grant permission. As soon as Aditya left, he called Lala.

'We need to meet at our usual spot. Immediately.'

Jayant reached a nondescript hotel. Lala was waiting in a room permanently booked by him.

Lala: 'What is it now, Sinha? Why the hurry?'

Jayant: 'A police party is raiding your house to arrest you.'

Lala: 'Rubbish. No one would dare. And on what charges?'

Jayant: 'A couple of your men have turned against you and agreed to be state witnesses.'

Lala laughed loudly—as if he'd heard the joke of the year.

Lala: 'You're a fool, Sinha. No man of mine would

dare go against me. Last time someone tried, I cut down his entire family in front of him. No one will cross me—as long as I'm alive.'

'Yes, Lala—you're absolutely right,' came a voice from behind.

Before Jayant could react, a shot was fired. Lala died instantly, confusion frozen on his face.

Jayant was frozen with fear. When the second shot didn't come, he slowly turned. Aditya was standing at the door with a gun.

But what petrified Jayant was the man who entered right after—Bhushan Bhai.

Bhushan: 'You look confused, Sinha.'

Jayant: 'I don't understand.'

Bhushan: 'Neither did this bastard when I tried talking sense into him. He wanted my seat—had muscle but no brain.'

Jayant: 'Since when are you and Aditya friends?'

Bhushan (smirking): 'We're not. He's my employee—just like Tripathi was. Just like *you* are. How do you think he got a posting in this city? I wanted him here. You always need an inside man in the police—it helps.'

Jayant: 'But… I was already your man.'

Bhushan sneered, 'Yes—a man who was also working for Lala. You think I didn't know? I've known for some time, you two-faced bastard. It made sense for Lala to approach you. Everyone knew you were my man. That way, he got an inside man in the police *and* in my gang.'

He paused before continuing.

'So I called Aditya. I never told anyone he worked for me—not even my own people. When he raided Lala's godown, you warned Lala. That confirmed you were working for him. So this time, Aditya fed you a phony story, and you led us straight to him.'

Jayant, trembling: 'What happens now? How will Aditya justify being here? If there's no evidence against Lala, how will he justify shooting him? And even if he does, Lala's gang will come after him for revenge!'

Bhushan (calmly): 'That won't be a problem. No one would speak against Lala while he was alive. Now that he's dead—we'll find plenty. And as for him being a target...'

He looked at Aditya.

'...that won't matter. Because he didn't kill Lala.'

He pointed at Jayant.

'You did.'

Before Jayant could process those words, Aditya fired at him with a foreign-made pistol, then placed the weapon in Lala's dead hand.

5

HITCHCOCK'S PROTÉGÉ

It was a spacious multi-storey building which nobody had bothered to name. It was supposed to be part of a much larger complex with nine more buildings to be constructed. However, due to slow demand, the developer had postponed the plan until all the flats in this building were sold. One of the main reasons the housing project struggled to attract buyers was its isolated location—on the outskirts of the city, about 200 metres off the main road. To add to that, the surrounding area resembled an entry-level jungle, giving it an overall creepy feel. More than a residential space, it looked like something straight out of a Ramsay Brothers' movie set.

Families avoided the place because it was a lonely stretch, and singles didn't want it as the flats were too big and expensive for single occupancy. Only a few investors who saw future potential had purchased units. One of them was my college friend Harpreet Singh, who lived abroad but had kindly offered me his flat until I found more suitable accommodation.

The building lacked basic amenities like a working elevator or a watchman, but that didn't bother me. I wanted to be a writer and was working on my first novel. The secluded surroundings actually suited me. I was making good progress—until the day I got new neighbours.

I lived on the fourth floor, which had four flats with a considerable common area, identical to the other levels. The eight-storey building had only two occupants so far—me and someone on the first floor. Then entered Mr and Mrs Dasani, a young couple in their late twenties or early thirties. They moved into the flat opposite mine, and as I was their only immediate neighbour—and roughly their age—I became acquainted with them fairly quickly.

They seemed nice, but something felt off. I couldn't quite place it, but the feeling lingered. I kept asking myself—*Why would someone bring his family to an isolated place like this?* But I never found an answer.

One Sunday Afternoon

It was a Sunday afternoon—though my Sundays looked no different from my Mondays or any other weekday. My routine remained the same throughout, except that others called it a holiday. I left my flat to walk to the nearby market, about a kilometre away, to buy groceries.

I was going down the stairs when I spotted Mr Dasani on the second floor, speaking to someone on his mobile. He had his back to me and didn't realise I was there. I was about to greet him when something suspicious stirred in my overactive mind—*What was he doing on this floor?* He could have taken the call on our floor. Was it a coincidence that he happened to be there when the call came, or did he deliberately come down to avoid being overheard?

He was speaking very softly—just above a whisper. But what he said froze me.

Mr Dasani: 'Day after tomorrow, I'll leave the house in the afternoon. I'll tell everyone I have to go to another city for two days for work. My wife will be alone. It's an isolated place; there's just one neighbour on my floor, but he usually keeps to himself. You'll have no problem. Come at night and finish the job. Nobody will ever know.'

My heart raced. I wanted to scream but couldn't. I silently turned around and sprinted back to my flat. I didn't want him to realise I had overheard the conversation.

Panicking, I called the only person I could think of—Vallabh Sisodiya, currently serving in the State Police Service and a college batchmate of both Harpreet and me.

Vallabh (sleepily): 'Who is this?'

Me: 'It's Alok, you idiot. Doesn't your caller ID work?'

Vallabh: 'It works fine, thank you. I was in the middle of an important case—meaning, my afternoon nap—so I didn't look at the screen.'

I quickly told him everything.

Vallabh: 'I understand you're currently writing a novel.'

Me: 'Yes.'

Vallabh: 'What's the genre?'

Me: 'Murder mystery.'

Vallabh (dryly): 'Take a couple of days' rest. Your imagination is working overtime. This isn't the first time you've come up with such dramatic nonsense.'

He was right. Even during college, I wanted to be a

writer, but like many geniuses, I was never recognised. To ensure I got proper attention, I sometimes drunkenly dialled my friends late at night to narrate story ideas. Unfortunately, these calls often coincided with their sleeping hours—hence, instead of applause, I received innovative abuses and, on occasion, physical reprimands.

But this time it was different.

Me: 'I'm not making it up. I know what I heard. He's planning to have his wife killed.'

Vallabh: 'I have a feeling you should be living far away from civilisation. Since that's legally impossible, Harpreet tricked you into living in a remote building, fulfilling his civic duty. As for why a young couple would move to an isolated area—my guess would be romance.'

Me: 'Well, the romance between Mr and Mrs Dasani died a premature death—just like Mrs Dasani is about to.'

Vallabh: 'Wait! A husband planning to have his wife murdered while establishing an alibi? Haven't I heard this before? Are you seriously narrating *Dial M for Murder?*'

Me: 'A man lends his flat to a friend, who witnesses a murder—it's more like *Body Double.*'

Vallabh: 'A neighbour suspects foul play, watches from across the building—you're one broken leg away from becoming James Stewart from *Rear Window.*'

We both laughed. Even with death looming next door, friends always find time to chuckle. I believe something to that effect is written in the Vedas. If it isn't—it should be.

On a serious note, he advised me to mind my own business and call only if I had *concrete evidence*. That evening and night, I tried to convince myself I had misheard. That everything was fine. That I wasn't a paranoid idiot. But I couldn't shake the feeling.

The next day, I visited the Dasanis to observe their household. When I saw Mrs Dasani deeply involved in preparing for her husband's upcoming trip, I could not wait any longer. I had to act. Sun Tzu aptly wrote in *The Art of War*, 'Protect thy neighbour', unless he is attacking you. If Tzu did not write it, he should have.

The writer inside me went into ninja mode. *What if I were planning this murder?* I listed the facts:

1. He brought his wife to an isolated location to avoid interference.

2. He would be out of town during the crime to establish an alibi.

The police would first ask—Why was she killed? Easy: A burglary gone wrong.

But would the murderer use a gun? No—too noisy. Knife? Yes. Silent and plausible.

Then—How would he enter? Doorbell? Risky. Perhaps a spare key, just like in *Dial M for Murder*.

This triggered a moment of self-doubt. *Was I really thinking originally, or was Vallabh right about my Hitchcock obsession?* But I was in too deep now to quit.

How could I prevent it? Warning her wouldn't work—who listens to a stranger over their spouse? Confronting the killer? Out of the question.

After hours of brainstorming, a half-baked plan emerged. Risky, with holes—but it was all I had.

The next afternoon, I saw Mr Dasani leave. I began.

There were four flats on my floor—401, 402, 403, 404. I lived in 403. They lived in 402.

Dasani lived in 402 and following was the floor plan:

<table>
<tr><td>Flat no 401</td><td>Flat no 402</td></tr>
<tr><td></td><td rowspan="3">Open Area</td></tr>
<tr><td>Stairs</td></tr>
<tr><td></td></tr>
<tr><td>Flat no 404</td><td>Flat no 403</td></tr>
</table>

Using a screwdriver, I swapped the number plates.

<table>
<tr><td>Flat no 404</td><td>Flat no 403</td></tr>
<tr><td></td><td rowspan="3">Open Area</td></tr>
<tr><td>Stairs</td></tr>
<tr><td></td></tr>
<tr><td>Flat no 401</td><td>Flat no 402</td></tr>
</table>

The idea was that the killer, using only flat numbers, would mistakenly enter *my* flat instead of theirs—unless he already knew the correct one.

In the evening, I visited Mrs Dasani and sat in her living room, watching the common area through the window. She gradually became less hospitable—perhaps annoyed by my prolonged presence or sensing something sinister.

Eventually, she excused herself to prepare dinner. I stayed put.

Suddenly, I heard footsteps. A tall man in dark clothing appeared—a film noir character come alive. He walked towards *my* flat. I had intentionally left the door unlocked; otherwise, the key wouldn't have fit.

I watched through the peephole, counting backwards under my breath.

'Ten… nine… eight… seven…'

He pushed the door open and entered.

At 'one,' I quietly stepped out of the Dasanis' flat and locked *my flat's door* from outside.

I had trapped him.

Just then, an angry-looking Mr Dasani stormed up the stairs. I hadn't accounted for backup. I thought it was over. Mrs Dasani and I were finished.

But what followed was insane.

Mr Dasani explained that he suspected his wife of infidelity. He had hired a private investigator to watch her, but the detective never found anything. So Dasani moved here to test her. He pretended to leave town and instructed the investigator to stay in one of the empty flats and observe.

But the investigator quit the assignment for a better-paying job.

Desperate not to waste the opportunity, Dasani himself returned early to catch her red-handed.

Instead, he found his wife's lover *locked* inside my flat.

The man had entered thinking it was her flat—thanks to my number swap. And Mrs Dasani had been uneasy with me earlier because she was waiting for him.

Dasani thanked me profusely for clarifying his doubts and requested I keep the matter private. He said he would seek marriage counselling. He even offered me money for my 'services,' which I politely declined.

After all, I had just found the plot for my next novel—complete with suspense, paranoia, comedy, mistaken identity and a twisted ending.

I hope Hitchcock would be proud.

6

THE LAST SUSPECT

Saturday Afternoon

It was a beautiful office—the kind where cheerful interiors complemented expensive furniture, and nobody really noticed. However, this sort of creativity was expected from an advertising firm. It was run by Mr Yashwardhan Tiwari, a middle-aged, soon-to-be bald man. 'Nostalgia' was the name of the firm.

It was a mid-level setup with a couple of assistants and seven copywriters. It was 4:30 pm on a Saturday afternoon, a half-day, and everyone was in a holiday spirit.

Amit Marwah was a young man in his late twenties—the best copywriter Tiwari had—and today was his birthday.

All the copywriters and Mr Tiwari were seated in the office canteen when it was decided that a small celebration was in order.

Amit said, 'Well, I need to go to my place to freshen up a little and pick up a wine bottle on my way back here. Somebody give me a lift to my house; I'll return on my own.'

There was a collective murmur among those present; nobody wanted to volunteer, as it was still hot outside. So Amit decided to choose a driver himself.

'So Gopal, will you do the honours?'

Gopal Krishnamurthy—a laid-back guy with a reputation for being a Casanova and a brat—gave a condescending smile and replied, 'No can do, brother. I have an important meeting. I'm heading there now, but I'll come back for the party in some time. Don't worry.'

Faizan Hussain, the serious guy with anger issues, had some work at his home, so he also left with an apology and a promise to attend the festivities later.

Amit now set his eyes on Chandrakant Awasthi, aka Chandru, who was a fox in every sense. Before Amit could bother him, Chandru diverted the threat.

Chandru said, 'Hey Bhavin, why don't you go with Amit? It will take no more than 40–45 minutes for a round trip.'

Bhavin Mehta, the junior-most and most obedient guy in the room, looked hopefully at the remaining two copywriters, Danny Samuels and Eshaan Lalwani. Both of them pretended to be in a deep conversation about earth-shattering issues.

Bhavin sighed and accompanied Amit toward the exit.

It was 5:30 pm when Mr Tiwari announced he had some important business to attend to and would return shortly. The remaining three people—Chandru, Danny and Eshaan—started playing cards.

Around 5:45 pm, Eshaan's phone started ringing.

Eshaan said, 'Hey, it's Amit. Let me ask him how much more time he needs.'

'Hello… hello…'

'Crap, looks like a bad connection. I can't understand what he's saying.'

Chandru said, 'Don't worry, he's calling me now.'

'Hi Amit, when will you come?'

For a few moments Chandru kept listening, then said, 'Okay… okay… fine.'

'Well, Amit says he'll reach the office in around 45 minutes,' Chandru informed the other two.

Danny said, 'Okay, looks like we can play a few more rounds till everyone comes back.'

Around 6:35 pm, Faizan entered the office, closely followed by Gopal.

Faizan said, 'Hey Gopal, didn't I spot you at Cheers Café at around 6 o'clock? I was on the other side of the road, and you were talking to someone, weren't you?'

Gopal gave a casual look around the canteen and replied, 'Oh yes, that was Amit. I was just coming out of the café when I saw him. He was returning to the office. He hasn't reached yet, has he?'

Chandru gave a suspicious look to Gopal and replied, 'No. We're still waiting for him.'

Mr Tiwari came back by 6:45 pm, but there was still no sign of Amit. His phone was also not reachable.

Everyone was getting worried. And then, suddenly, the police arrived.

Saturday Night, 10.00 pm

Amit Marwah's body was found behind the building he lived in. That section was rarely used, so not many people went in that direction. Around 8:00 pm on Saturday, someone went there to smoke a cigarette when he noticed the body.

From its condition, it was clear that Amit had fallen from the terrace of the seven-floor building. The time of death was still undecided until the police located the office where Amit worked.

The police were reluctant to give an opinion on whether it was an accident, suicide, or murder.

Vasudev, aka Vasu Agrawal, was in charge of the investigation. He was in his late twenties, with inquisitive eyes and a mischievous expression on his face.

He started his enquiries with Mr Tiwari.

Vasu: 'We found fresh cigarette butts and ash on the terrace. Most certainly Amit was having a puff there. He may have fallen by accident or may have committed suicide—we can't be sure at this point.'

Tiwari gave an uncomfortable expression, which Vasu didn't miss. 'What is bothering you, Mr Tiwari?'

Tiwari: 'You didn't mention murder.'

Vasu stared intensely and replied, 'Could it be murder? Come on, what are you not telling me?'

Tiwari sighed. 'Well... my business is all right, but of late I've realised that I don't require seven copywriters. I can very well do my work with six.'

Vasu: 'So you were thinking of firing someone. Did your people know? Was it Amit you were about to let go?'

Tiwari: 'Yes, they knew. And no—I wasn't going to fire Amit. He was the best of the lot. On the contrary, he resigned. He got a better offer and was about to move on.'

Vasu: 'So what's the problem? The others would have

been relieved—the six remaining ones, I mean. But that would have meant letting go of a good performer and being left with inferior talent.'

Sensing the accusation in the police officer's tone, Tiwari quickly replied, 'No, that's not the case. It's very common in our line of work—people come and go. In fact, yesterday he told me he had decided to stay with Nostalgia. I readily agreed.'

A twinkle appeared in Vasu's eye. 'That means you would have to sack one of the remaining guys. That's a solid motive—with six potential suspects. Did the others know about it?'

Tiwari: 'To my knowledge, nobody else except Amit and I knew. It would have caused panic, and I didn't want that today.'

Vasu: 'Nevertheless, tell me the movements of everyone present here since the time Amit left the building.'

Vasu took statements from all six copywriters one by one in Mr Tiwari's office.

Danny: 'I don't know, man. I was here the whole time. Never left the building. Ask Eshaan or Chandru—they were with me the whole time. Eshaan even received a call from Amit around quarter to six.'

Chandru: 'Yes, Danny is right. All three of us were here all the time. And yes, Eshaan got the call from Amit. Then Amit called me and said he would be coming to the office in about 45 minutes—that meant we were expecting him around 6:30 pm. He never showed up.'

Eshaan corroborated the statements given by Chandru and Danny.

Faizan: 'I had some work at my home, so I left the office around 4:30 pm. I returned at around 6:20 pm.'

Vasu: 'Where do you live? How far is your house from this office?'

Faizan: 'I live in Saket Colony. It's about 15 minutes away by two-wheeler.'

Gopal: 'Well, honestly, I had a date. I waited for her at Cheers Café for more than an hour. She never came—as girls sometimes do. Anyway, around 6:00 pm, I came out of the café and ran into Amit. He said he was returning to the office from home.'

After their respective statements, everyone was waiting in the canteen when Vasu entered.

Vasu: 'All right, I got all your statements. But one person is missing—Bhavin, the guy who left with Amit in the afternoon. Where the hell is he?'

Suddenly, there was silence in the room, and doubt started creeping into many minds. Bhavin had left with Amit and had been missing since then. It made everyone uncomfortable.

Just then, Chandru shouted, 'I just received a call from Bhavin! He got into an accident and is at General Hospital now.'

General Hospital

Vasu reached the hospital and asked for the doctor in charge of Bhavin. The doctor told him that Bhavin had been involved in a minor accident when his two-wheeler slipped on the road. He was suffering from minor bruises and a hairline fracture—nothing serious.

At Vasu's insistence, the doctor checked the admission form, which clearly stated that Bhavin had been admitted to the hospital at around 5:20 pm.

Police Station, Sunday Morning

Vasu was sitting in his chair at the police station, a little dozy from the previous night. He called for his junior, Shashank Kathuria, who was taking care of combing the area where Amit's body was found.

Vasu: 'Tell me, what did you find at the spot?'

Kathuria: 'Nothing you didn't already know. He had his purse in his pocket, some personal identification papers, a little cash—nothing extraordinary. Anyway, what's your reading of the case?'

Vasu became alert, as if recollecting all the vital facts in his mind: 'Okay, there are a total of eight people involved in this case that we know of so far—one is Amit, the victim; one is his boss, Mr Tiwari; and six colleagues. Amit never interacted with his neighbours and didn't have a family. So the suspects are limited to his co-workers.'

'Anyway, Amit left his office at 4:30 pm on Saturday with his colleague Bhavin, closely followed by his other colleagues, Gopal and Faizan. At 5:30 pm, Mr Tiwari, the owner of the business, left the building, while Chandru, Danny, and Eshaan remained in the office and never left the premises.'

'At 6:35 pm, Faizan and Gopal returned to the office, and Mr Tiwari came back at 6:45 pm.'

'Amit called Eshaan and Chandru at the office around 5:45 pm. He didn't give his location but said he would arrive in 45 minutes. Then he met Gopal at Cheers Café at about 6:00 pm, while returning to the office. His body was discovered at 8:00 pm.'

Kathuria: 'How far is the office from Amit's house?'

Vasu: 'Let me draw a diagram for you.'

Vasu: 'It takes about 20 minutes to cover the distance between their office and Amit's building. Cheers Café is halfway between the two, so 10 minutes from the office to the café and 10 minutes from the café to the building.' He stopped to take a deep breath and continued, 'So let's say at 6:00 pm, Amit was at the café. It would take 10 minutes to reach his building, so he reaches the building at 6:10 pm, gets thrown off from the roof, which may have taken around 5 minutes, so it's 6:15 pm now. Then the killer goes back to the office, which took another 20 minutes, meaning by 6:35 pm.'

Kathuria: 'But Amit was returning to the office. Why would he go back to his house?'

Vasu: 'It's a valid point. Maybe he suddenly remembered something and went back, or maybe someone asked him to go back with them.'

Kathuria: 'Okay, let's go with that hypothesis for a while. So the killer would have reached the office by 6:35 pm, which means Faizan, Gopal, and Tiwari—all three—could have made it just in the nick of time.'

Vasu: 'Faizan and Gopal had motive, but what about Tiwari? He didn't have any; Amit was his best man and was staying with him. Why would he kill him?'

Kathuria: 'How do you know Amit was going to stay? You only have Tiwari's word on that. They never told anybody. So the whole thing could have been Tiwari's doing—pissed at Amit for leaving, he kills him and makes up a story that implicates others.'

Kathuria had a point, and Vasu had to concede: even Tiwari could have a motive just like the others.

Vasu: 'Okay, agree about Tiwari, but let's talk about

opportunity. Three people were at the office all the time—Chandru, Danny, and Eshaan. We have cross-verified that with other sources, like the security officer posted outside the building, who insisted there was no other way to leave the building and no way anyone could pass without his noticing. So we can leave these three out for now.'

'Second, the killer must have known that Amit would be present at his building when he reached there. How could the killer have known that? Let's talk about Gopal: he was at Cheers Café meeting some girl when he accidentally bumped into Amit, who told him he was on his way to the office. So Gopal couldn't have known that Amit would then turn back to his building.'

'Faizan spotted Gopal from the other side of the road. He saw Gopal outside Cheers Café talking to someone but couldn't identify the other person. He actually asked Gopal whom he was talking to when they both reached the office. He didn't know it was Amit until Gopal told him, so he couldn't have known either.'

Kathuria: 'What about Bhavin? He went with Amit to his building. Maybe he pushed him?'

Vasu: 'Yes, he had the opportunity, but the timing didn't match. Bhavin was admitted to a hospital at 5:20 pm, much before Amit was killed. The more I think about it, the more I believe it was not a killing—either a suicide or an accident.'

Kathuria was still uncomfortable, unconvinced, and unrelenting: 'What about Tiwari?'

Vasu: 'Well, how could Tiwari have known about Amit's movements? How would he have known to find Amit at his building?'

Kathuria: 'Maybe he called him?'

Vasu: 'Maybe. So check Amit's phone and find all the call details so we can know for sure.'

Kathuria replied apologetically: 'Sir, we are still trying to locate the victim's mobile. We searched the area, but it was dark. The mobile could have dropped nearby.'

Vasu gave a sigh: 'Well, then please search the area again in daylight.'

Nostalgia, Sunday Afternoon

Vasu entered the office to find the staff sitting in the canteen, sipping coffee. The wine that Amit had promised was a distant dream. As soon as they saw Vasu, they leapt toward him.

Tiwari asked inquiringly: 'Sir, any progress? Do you know what happened?'

Vasu shook his head and replied: 'It's early days; we are still investigating. However, are you generally open on a Sunday?'

Faizan replied condescendingly: 'It's not every Sunday you lose a co-worker and a friend.'

Danny: 'Technically, it was a Saturday, but I believe the policeman gets what you are trying to tell him.'

Vasu: 'Of course I do, and I apologise for being insensitive. So everyone is here except, I believe, Gopal and Chandru.'

Eshaan: 'Yes, Gopal has been a nervous wreck since yesterday and is currently dealing with his anxiety inside the toilet. Chandru has gone to the hospital since morning to meet Bhavin, who, if I may point out, is also not here.'

Vasu ignored the sly remark on his observational abilities and tried to protect the remainder of his dignity by pretending to be all businesslike: 'Why has only Chandru gone to meet Bhavin? Why no one else?'

'Well, Bhavin is kind of a protégé to Chandru. Well, we all are, but as they say, 'some animals are more equal than others'—kind of a situation,' replied Danny, quoting *Animal Farm*, believing its significance would not be lost on Vasu—which, in fact, it was.

Before Vasu could continue, which looked more like his interrogation than the other way around, he received an important call from Kathuria, giving him two crucial pieces of information: first, the investigators found Amit's phone near the bushes where he was discovered; and second, there were no fingerprints on the phone.

Police Station

Vasu rushed to the station. Kathuria was waiting anxiously with all the details.

Vasu: 'That was quick work, Kathuria.'

Kathuria: 'Thanks. As soon as our people reached the spot, they discovered the phone in the nearby bushes. It was odd because they swear that last time they had thoroughly checked that area. I felt a little uneasy and immediately sent it for forensic testing. The result came back immediately: there were no fingerprints on the phone, not even partial, meaning the mobile had been wiped clean.'

Vasu: 'Let's visit the spot again.'

Vasu and Kathuria were standing on the less-used side of the building where Amit's body was found. First, looking toward the roof and slowly turning his gaze toward the ground, Vasu said, 'There is no way a mobile hitting the ground from that height would suffer no damage!'

Kathuria: 'Exactly. The killer took the mobile with him after the murder, then panicked, cleaned his fingerprints, and threw the phone back into this area at the first chance he got, before our search party came here today.'

Vasu concurred. Both of them decided to visit Nostalgia.

It was on the way from Amit's building to Amit's office that Vasu spotted Cheers Café, and a realisation hit him like a ton of bricks.

Nostalgia

Vasu stormed into the office and ordered Gopal to join him and Kathuria in Mr Tiwari's office for a private chat.

Vasu: 'So, I've heard you are suffering from anxiety. What's the matter?'

Gopal: 'You know, our colleague died yesterday. It kind of creeps you out.'

Vasu: 'Even when you yourself killed him?'

Gopal's face flushed, but his voice suddenly took on a pinched quality that could even raise the dead. 'What in hell's name are you talking about? Are you mad, officer?'

Vasu: 'You told your colleagues and the police that you met Amit when he was returning to the office outside Cheers Café, but that café is on the wrong side of the road. If you are going from the office to Amit's building, only then is the cafe on your route. When you are returning from Amit's building to the office, you need to take the parallel road—the same road from where Faizan saw you. It means Amit was actually going toward the building when you met him, you went with him to his building, pushed him, and came back to the office.'

Gopal remained speechless for some time and then, with considerable effort, started speaking in a slow voice: 'I knew this was going to bite me in the ass. I'm sorry, officer. I lied to you all. I never met Amit outside the café.'

Vasu was taken aback but kept his cool: 'Then why did you say you did, and whom were you talking to outside the café?'

The embarrassment on Gopal's face was quite visible. 'I was meeting a girl there—she is Faizan's sister. He didn't know, of course; nobody knew. I was with her when I left the café, and I was talking to her when Faizan spotted me. He questioned me in the office, and I panicked. I looked around and saw that Amit was not there, so I lied that I met him. I thought I would convince him as soon as he returned to back my story. But that didn't happen. I didn't know at the time that my lie would become legal testimony. When the inquiry started, I was unable to retract my statement. I was under tremendous pressure for all the mess I created, and that's why I am anxious about a lot of things.'

With those words, Gopal started sobbing.

Police Station

It was a setback; the perfect theory had gone to dust. Vasu had a chat with the employees of Cheers, and Gopal's story had checked out so far. He made a mental note to interview Faizan's sister without creating much fuss. He knew why Gopal had lied, because the situation, if mishandled, could have resulted in anything, from manhandling to a small riot.

Vasu was resisting the temptation of lighting a cigarette. He rarely smoked, but the situation warranted some relaxation, so he lit one and started drawing deep clouds of smoke. It was then that Kathuria entered his cabin with some papers. When he saw his boss in this mood, he started to turn back.

Vasu: 'What is it, Kathuria? Why are you going back?'

Kathuria: 'Nothing important, Sir. I can come back; it's just the information you asked for.'

Vasu: 'What information?'

Kathuria: 'Well, you said you wanted the call records of all the people involved in the case. The information has just been received and compiled by us.'

Vasu: 'Ah, I never meant all the call records. I was interested in just Amit's phone. It's a waste of resources, I tell you. Did you find anything useful?'

Kathuria: 'It's as dull as an art movie. Nobody called anybody—just one call from Amit to Eshaan and one to Chandru, nothing else.'

'It's a talkative bunch, this lot,' Vasu said sarcastically. Suddenly, his facial expression changed. Kathuria noticed and decided to withhold all further communication with his boss until Vasu was ready to talk.

It took a few minutes, then suddenly a knowing smile appeared on Vasu's face. The case had been cracked.

Nostalgia

Everyone was present at the beautiful office of Nostalgia: Vasu, Kathuria, Tiwari, and all the copywriters, including Bhavin, who had returned from the hospital.

Vasu: 'So, Bhavin, how are you feeling?'

Bhavin: 'All right, Sir. Feeling much better, thank you.'

Vasu: 'So what happened—the accident, I mean?'

Bhavin: 'Well, it was my mistake, I believe. I took a sharp turn, couldn't control the vehicle, and some kind people took me to the hospital.'

Vasu: 'Then from the hospital, you called Faizan, I believe?'

Bhavin: 'No, Sir. I called Chandru.'

Vasu gave a knowing smile, raised the papers he was carrying—these were the call details of all the members of Nostalgia—and said, 'Yes, I believe that's what Chandru said in his statement as well. Then will you care to explain why there is no record of such a call, neither as an outgoing call from your mobile nor as a received call on Chandru's mobile?'

There was silence for a moment.

Vasu continued, 'That means no such call was ever made regarding Bhavin's hospitalisation. Then how did Chandru know Bhavin was in General Hospital? There was only one way: the call received by Chandru, supposed to be from Amit, was actually from Bhavin.'

Suddenly, Chandru and Bhavin became uncomfortable. The police had cracked the case, and realising their game was over, they let out a sigh of defeat.

Bhavin confessed to killing Amit. Here's what happened: After leaving the office at 4:30 pm, Bhavin went with Amit to his building, where Amit asked Bhavin to join him on the terrace for a smoke. There, uncharacteristically out of guilt, Amit told Bhavin about his decision to continue with the firm. This enraged Bhavin; he took it as a betrayal, as it affected his own employment with Nostalgia. In the spur of the moment, he pushed Amit to his death. It was 4:55 pm.

After a few moments, when his nerves calmed down, Bhavin started forming a plan. But he needed an accomplice. He took Amit's phone with him, which had been left behind on the roof. He then caused a minor accident intentionally and got himself hospitalised by 5:20 pm, thereby creating an alibi that he had been at the hospital since then.

Next, he called Eshaan through Amit's phone but created disturbances so his voice would remain unidentifiable. This created the illusion that Amit was calling Eshaan, and due to a bad connection, he then called Chandru.

Chandru was the only friend and chance Bhavin had. It was a gamble, but he had to play it; there was no other way. Bhavin told Chandru about Amit's 'betrayal' and asked him to play along. Now there were two witnesses, Eshaan and Chandru, who had allegedly talked with Amit at 5:45 pm. Bhavin was safe, as it was established that by 5:20 pm, he was already hospitalised.

The next morning, when Chandru went to visit Bhavin, he took Amit's mobile from him and dropped it at the spot where Amit was found.

What complicated things for the police—and worked in Bhavin's favour—was Gopal's statement that he met Amit at 6:00 pm. Chandru was surprised, as he had no idea that Gopal was just trying to save his own ass.

7

FOR LOVE OR MONEY

(i)

What do young guys talk about nowadays when they are alone? Well, the same stuff they've been talking about for decades—women—and they've never been able to reach any conclusion on the topic, because the people who might have answers are either dead or married, so in either case, they can't open their mouths.

In the present case too, two college friends are debating the true and deeper meaning of love.

Anadi: 'Are you kidding? You really believe that?'

Sameer: 'What's there not to believe? I have seen it, and so have many other people. Money and love are two separate things—you don't need the former to have the latter.'

Anadi: 'You think like a girl. Even girls nowadays are practical. They won't go out with you if you're not seriously rich. A poor guy gets the consolation prize of being a good friend, and the rich one wins consistently, even if he's not contesting.'

Sameer: 'My girl will never do that to me.'

Anadi: 'First, you need a girl for that, you moron. I bet no girl would ever consider a serious relationship with a guy who has empty pockets.'

Sameer: 'I accept your bet. Whenever I find a girlfriend, she will love me for who I am—nothing else.'

Anadi: 'You're my best friend. I hope to lose this bet, but you know what? I won't.'

(ii)

The new academic year started a few months after this conversation, and the wheels of fate were set into motion with the entry of a new girl—Shruti. A girl any guy would easily and willingly fall for. An Indian beauty with sharp features, someone who looked equally stunning in western as well as Indian attire. The way she carried herself made every guy's heart skip a beat.

Sameer was no exception, but he was reluctant to approach her, assuming many guys must have already done the needful. Not that he wasn't good-looking or confident, but rejection or outright humiliation in the middle of campus—is never good for self-esteem.

He approached her anyway, with enough courage, and said, 'Well, I thought of a lot of cheesy lines, but I guess I'm not good at that stuff, so I'll ask you directly — would you like to have a cup of coffee with me at a really nice cafe just around the corner? It's nearby, so you can walk back here in case you don't like me or the coffee.'

Shruti gave a careful look at Sameer from top to bottom and said with a hint of a smile, 'Not bad for a start. Honesty is underrated, but I wouldn't mind taking a chance.'

Shruti didn't walk out on Sameer, or even the coffee. Sameer, being the gentleman, behaved with perfect decorum, paid the bill, and even dropped her home on his bike. Not bad for the first date.

(iii)

In the following days, Sameer got to know a lot about Shruti and her family. He liked her voice, so instead of talking about himself, he preferred listening to her. He tried hard to impress her by all means possible—movies, dinners, and the occasional gifts.

Anadi was watching all this from a distance and never interfered. He himself was unsure about the bet he had made with Sameer, who by now may have even forgotten it. But for Anadi, it wasn't about the bet anymore—it was about his friend, his choices, and the repercussions that might follow.

Anadi: 'So, how's it going between you two?'

Sameer: 'Excellent! I've found the girl of my dreams. I'm serious about her. I'm going to tell my parents about her.'

Anadi: 'Aren't you going too fast? Have you even asked her?'

Sameer: 'I don't need to ask her. I can see it in her eyes—she wouldn't say no, I'm sure. And I'll make sure she never regrets it.'

Anadi took a moment before saying, 'Do you remember our little bet from some time back?'

Sameer gave him a sceptical look, 'Are you still hung up on that? You think she could dump me for money?'

Anadi: 'I don't know, man. But you haven't given her the chance to. You two go to good restaurants, movies every week, you give her gifts — not to mention your bike, which only a few boys in college can afford.'

Sameer: 'What are you suggesting?'

Anadi: 'Why don't you bring your father tomorrow so she can meet him—and more importantly, he can meet her? Not to mention, have you even told her what your father does?'

Sameer: 'No... I haven't discussed my parents with her. (Suddenly, Sameer understood what Anadi was suggesting.)'

(iv)

The next day, Shruti dressed in the best possible way. Sameer's father was coming to college to meet her. She looked stunning—no one could have imagined saying no to a girl like her.

Sameer missed the expression in Shruti's eyes when he told her that his father works as a senior clerk at a government bank—as well as the disgust when she saw the scooter his father was riding.

It didn't take more than a week for the breakup. As soon as he proposed to her, she replied that she saw him as just a good friend, nothing more. Sameer got his consolation prize. The following week, she started going out with another guy whose father owned a small business and earned much more than a bank clerk.

Anadi took care of his friend, ensuring he didn't do anything stupid. But revenge was due—and the counter-attack would be his.

It was the day of the last exam for the first-year students. Anadi was waiting in the corridor for Shruti to exit the exam hall. What a year it had been for his friend. When Shruti arrived, he asked for a quick word.

Shruti: 'I'm afraid I have nothing to say about the matter. It's over. I never considered him anything more than a friend—he had the wrong impression.'

Anadi: 'I know it's over. I'm not here to talk about that. I just wanted to say that you did consider him more than a friend but threw him under the bus as soon as you realised he wasn't as rich as you thought. Please don't deny it—I don't want to fight. You see, I made a bet with my friend that a girl likes a boy for his money more than anything else. So if that's true, it means I've won, and it will teach him a lesson for the future. You can at least be honest one time.'

Shruti: 'You talk about honesty. Yes, I dumped him for that reason, but he hadn't been honest with me either. He gave the impression that he was rich—his clothes, his accessories, his bike were all expensive, the restaurants we went to were high-end. But how could he afford them if his father is just a bank clerk? It means he was pretending to be rich at his father's expense! His father must have taken loans, exhausted his savings so his son could have a good life.

'And you expect me to buy into this lie? I was born in a middle-class family, but I don't want to remain in the same condition for the rest of my life. So if anyone did something wrong, it was your friend.'

After a moment of silence, Anadi said, 'You know something—you're right. A guy pretending to be something he's not is also unacceptable. But let me tell you a story...

'About 30 years ago, a girl fell in love with a simple guy. He wasn't rich but had unblemished integrity. When she told her father—Mr Agarwal, a big businessman—he met the boy and agreed to the marriage. The boy, even after marrying a wealthy woman, retained his job. He always said he married the girl, not her money or business. That integrity was the reason her father chose him in the first place.

'That man still works in the same office. And if you haven't guessed already—that man is Sameer's father. So even though he is a clerk, his son isn't poor by inheritance. His wealth comes from his mother, who is considered one of the richest women in the city. So you see—Sameer wasn't pretending to be rich. He is filthy rich.'

Shruti's face suddenly turned pale—it looked like she couldn't breathe. Realising his counter-strike had worked, Anadi walked away slowly, saying aloud, 'You know something—I always knew I would win this bet, because love was rare back then. Now... it's fake.'

8

ALL HAIL THE KING

(i)

The clock showed 7:30 pm. Another working day had ended for middle-aged Damodar Thakur who worked for a pharmaceutical company. Damodar's life was monotonous and followed the same routine. He would leave his office by 7:45 pm, stroll to the nearby bus stand, reach home by 8:30 pm, make his own dinner, go to sleep and return to the office in the morning. For him, thrill and adventure were like those rich distant relatives who existed but never came near. But today, the routine was about to be broken.

While Damodar was walking towards the bus stand, he sensed someone following him. He dismissed the thought immediately, telling himself that such things happened only in spy thrillers, not in real life. Why would anybody bother to follow him? Even a pickpocket wouldn't get much out of his purse. However, he was proved wrong instantaneously when two men wearing black suits approached him from both sides. Damodar felt a chill run down his spine as one of them spoke, 'Mr Thakur, you need to accompany us.' Damodar was too terrified to speak; he just nodded.

He found himself sitting in the back seat of a luxury vehicle. A million thoughts ran through his head. However, when the car arrived at the doors of the most prestigious hotel in the city—instead of a dark alley as he had imagined—he felt somewhat relieved. He was escorted to a suite on the top floor. When the door opened, Damodar saw an elderly man present inside. The man was impeccably dressed and exuded professionalism. As he looked at Damodar with piercing eyes, Damodar felt uneasy—though to be frank, he had been uneasy since the moment he was picked up by the two strangers. The man asked the two men to leave and gestured for Damodar to sit.

Without delay, the man began speaking. 'My name is Shankar Deewan,' he said. 'I am the official representative of Larka Islands on behalf of His Highness Shri Veer Vikram Singhji, the king of Larka Island.' Damodar had little use for this information. What he couldn't understand was why a country—or an island—would want to kidnap him. Sensing the confusion, Shankar continued, 'We would like to engage your services on behalf of our country.'

Damodar replied, 'Well, Sir, I believe you're mistaken. I am a common man; I work for a pharmaceutical company as a lab assistant. I don't think I can be of any help. Maybe you've picked the wrong guy.'

Deewan managed a slight smile. 'No, Damodar, we haven't made any mistakes. We've been observing you for over a year now. Of course, you don't know what we want from you—that's why you look perplexed. So, let me put it simply: would you like to earn so much money in a few months that it would be sufficient to take care of your every need for the rest of your life?'

Damodar, half expecting the offer to be true, asked apprehensively, 'What do you want me to do, Mr Deewan?'

With a wider smile, Deewan said, 'I want you to become the King of Larka Island, Damodar.'

(ii)

As Damodar processed the information, Shankar Deewan was staring at him with a cigar in his hand. Damodar asked, 'Is this a joke, Mr Deewan? It is a terrible prank to play on a simple man like me. Have some fear of God and tell me the truth.'

Deewan was taken aback. Being the kind of man accustomed to being taken seriously, this felt like an insult. His voice now carried a hint of rudeness. 'Look around you, Mr Thakur—the luxurious room you're in, the expensive car you were brought in. Hell, look at me. Do you really believe you're important enough for someone to spend this kind of effort to play a prank on you?'

Deewan was right, and Damodar knew it. It was not a joke.

Damodar gathered himself. 'Okay, what do you want me to do?'

Deewan resumed his professional tone. 'Well, the King of Larka Island, His Highness Shri Veer Vikram Singhji, needs to travel to a foreign country for a surgical procedure. The operation and recovery will take months, and we cannot afford for the crown to be vacant for that long.'

Damodar asked, 'Meaning?'

'Meaning, if the King is away that long, it will give the rebels an opportunity to strike. We don't want them to know that our King is not on the island.'

Damodar looked puzzled. 'I'm still confused. What does that have to do with me? Where do I fit in?'

Deewan replied, 'You fit right on the throne, my friend. Oh—did I forget to mention? You look exactly like our King, His Highness Shri Veer Vikram Singhji. We want you to pose as him while he is away.'

And once again, the room fell silent.

(iii)

The next day, Damodar left for Larka Island with Shankar Deewan. It turned out that during Deewan's last trip to India, he had spotted Damodar and had kept an eye on him ever since, in case of any emergency—and the emergency had now arrived. The offer was too generous to refuse, even at the risk of being killed by rebels. The only consolation was that lynching had gone out of fashion in the 1960s, though guns and bombs were still very much 'in'.

During the journey, Deewan gave Damodar details about the island. Before Veer Vikram Singh, his father, the late Ranjit Vikram Singh, was king. Larka Island had extensive natural resources, and crude oil was extracted by American companies, resulting in tremendous wealth.

After reaching the island, Damodar was secretly taken to the royal residence. No one but Deewan knew about him. For the first time, he saw the man identical to him in every aspect—His Highness Shri Veer Vikram Singhji.

Veer Vikram: 'I hope you had a pleasant trip.'

Damodar: 'Yes, Your Highness.'

Veer Vikram: 'Oh, come on. You don't need to call me that. I don't like being addressed formally. I was educated in the USA—I'm very liberal for a king.'

Neither Damodar nor Deewan responded. Veer Vikram continued, 'Okay, you don't need to worry about anything. All official work and decision-making will be handled by Deewanji. No one outside this room should ever know about this arrangement. I don't trust anybody.'

Damodar hesitantly asked, 'If you don't mind me asking, what's the problem with the rebels? You seem like a capable administrator, so why do you have rebellion on the island?'

Veer Vikram thought for a moment before replying. 'Well, to be honest, there's no country in the world—whether democratic, communist, socialist, or even monarchical—where everyone is satisfied with the government. So we also have a small group opposing us. And of course, we don't want to encourage them by telling them the country will be without its head for so long. That's where you come in. And don't worry—we have capable people guarding us. In the event of direct conflict, they don't stand a chance.'

That very evening, Veer Vikram Singh left for Japan.

(iv)

Damodar was given proper instructions about the daily routine. It was easy enough—Veer Vikram Singh had no immediate family, so that part was covered. All Damodar had to do was appear at events and avoid conversations. The arrangement worked well until something unexpected happened: Shankar Deewan suffered a fatal heart attack. This triggered a chain of events with unforeseen consequences.

The first to be affected was Damodar—his only ally was gone, and he didn't know what to do. As if that wasn't enough, the evening brought more bad news. Captain Hamish Khan, Head of Internal Security, arrived at the royal residence for an emergency meeting.

Hamish Khan: 'Your Highness, the news of Deewanji's death has spread across the island. The rebels are planning something big. They know Deewanji was too important for the kingdom and that his death weakens us. What are your instructions?'

Damodar felt his heart leap to his throat. He couldn't reveal that the empire was much weaker than expected, so he composed himself and countered, 'What are our options, Captain?'

Hamish Khan: 'We can attempt peace talks with their leader, as your father did on previous occasions. Or we can go offensive with direct raids.'

Damodar remembered what Veer Vikram had said about the outcome of direct conflict and immediately made up his mind. 'Captain, put the security forces on red alert. Declare curfew across the island and increase patrolling. Place additional security around the crude oil drilling site. If anyone attempts anything suspicious, show no mercy.'

Captain Hamish Khan, who had served loyally for decades under the previous king, had always seen conflicts resolved peacefully. This aggressive stance was unsettling, but he chose to remain silent. He nodded and left.

(v)

The situation was brought under control within a couple of days. The strategy worked. Intense patrolling and several instances of brutal security action rapidly demotivated the rebels. The battle was won before it began. Captain Hamish Khan returned with good news.

Captain: 'Your Highness, the situation is fully under control. The rebels were not prepared for the attack. Our timely action turned the tide in our favour.'

A now-confident Damodar replied, with borderline arrogance, 'Good work, Captain. And what peace talks were you speaking about? This is how problems are dealt with. Make sure there are no further uprisings. Do whatever necessary—apply extreme force if required. Tell them who's the boss... no, tell them who's the king.'

The captain noticed an obvious change in behaviour. He sighed, knowing the monarchy was turning into a dictatorship.

Over the next few days, Damodar continued crushing anything he considered anti-administration, resulting in innocent people being tortured and numerous human rights violations. The people of Larka Island were too stunned to react. In the process, Damodar had seized complete control of the island.

(vi)

One night, as Damodar was preparing to sleep, he received an important call—from the real king.

Veer Vikram: 'What is happening on the island, Damodar? You should have informed me about the situation. And what's this I'm hearing about violence? Have you lost your mind?'

Damodar: 'Watch your tone. Do you know who you're talking to? I am the king—don't insult me.'

Veer Vikram: 'Are you drunk? What are you talking about? You're not the king—I am!'

Damodar: 'Agreed, but who will believe that? No one besides you and me know the truth. The only person who could have saved you is already dead. There's no way you can prove you're the real king. If you come back to this island, I'll call you an imposter and hang you in the town square. So, for your own sake, stay away. You're educated abroad—you should know when you're defeated.'

Veer Vikram knew Damodar was right.

Damodar continued, 'You're an idiot, Veer Vikram Singh. You don't know how power works. Crush anyone in your way—you should have done it years ago. You wasted time on peace processes. Take a lesson from me and avoid being crushed yourself.'

Veer Vikram was indeed a smart man. He already had a large amount of money stashed in Swiss bank accounts. He had made provisions long ago in case he ever needed to leave the island—though not under these circumstances.

Veer Vikram: 'Okay, I will never return. But before I hang up, I want to thank you.'

Damodar, stunned: 'Thank me? For what? For ruining you? Are you insane?'

Veer Vikram: 'No, Damodar. Thank you for saving my skin.'

Damodar: 'I don't understand.'

Veer Vikram: 'Do you think you're the first person corrupted by power? No, my friend. Years ago, when I became king, I was like you—rash and unreasonable. When

I discovered a group of rebels hiding in a forest planning an uprising, I had it secretly burned down. All of them died. To this day, no one knows I did it—they think it was a forest fire.' Veer paused. 'But then I realised what a terrible mistake I'd made. I had become a murderer. The guilt consumed me. I tried to make amends and talk people out of violence, but it was too late. I had committed my sin.'

Damodar: 'Why are you telling me this? So what if you burned it? That won't affect me. I can handle the rebels—you said so yourself.'

Veer Vikram: 'Yes, you can defeat rebels in battle. But you will lose if the general public joins them—even half the security force will join if they know the truth. What you don't know is that the American drilling company had its site near that forest. Naturally, they couldn't afford a fire there, so they investigated and instantly determined it was manmade. They've been blackmailing me since—forcing me to sell crude at cheaper prices. I haven't slept properly since. You know how Americans are—they dislike dictatorships and monarchies. Bad for business. Look at the recent uprisings in the Middle East—each supported by the USA. It's only a matter of time before they decide Larka Island needs new leadership. And no uprising ends without a decapitated head of state. And since you are there—it certainly won't be mine.

'And one final note—if I were you, I'd start taking the sleeping pills from the cupboard. You'll need them every night from now on.'

The call ended, leaving Damodar speechless. He hung up and slowly walked towards the cupboard containing the sleeping pills.

9

REVENGE

(i)

It was 9:30 am on a Monday, and the office of *Kapoor Industries* was buzzing with activity. Prabhakar Reddy, the personal assistant to Mr Kapoor, was going through his routine work at his desk when Mr Kapoor entered the office.

Prabhakar: 'Good morning, Sir. Today you have a meeting with the promoters of Shakti Builders, then with your old friend and ex-partner Shri Raghav Bahal, and then—'

Kapoor cut him short. 'Wait a second. Why am I meeting Raghav?' he asked, clearly not too enthusiastic about seeing an old friend.

Prabhakar: 'Sir, our contract with his firm is about to expire. He requested an appointment to discuss the terms and conditions for the renewal.'

Kapoor: 'That bastard! Yes, I know. I don't want to see him—that blood-sucking cockroach.'

Prabhakar knew better than to question his boss's ill feelings towards an old friend. Never interrupting the boss was the golden rule, and this was just one of the many traits that helped Prabhakar rise rapidly in the company, earning his current position as Mr Kapoor's most trusted employee and adviser.

Kapoor continued, 'I should have terminated the contract years ago.'

Prabhakar: 'But instead, you've renewed it every time it became due.'

Kapoor: 'I know. I'm not gaining anything from this contract, but it's more of a silent deal between me and Raghav.'

Without waiting for Prabhakar to respond, Kapoor continued, 'Years ago, just after I finished my education and started my own business, I had the potential but not enough capital. So, I went into partnership with Raghav and Sunil.'

Prabhakar: 'I don't think you've ever told me anything about Sunil before—just that Raghav was an old business associate.'

Before Kapoor could reply, the intercom buzzed. The receptionist informed him that representatives from Shakti Builders had arrived and were waiting. Kapoor wanted to continue speaking but knew he shouldn't keep his business associates waiting. Prabhakar was relieved, assuming that Kapoor's story would eventually unfold—as it always did. Kapoor told Prabhakar to visit their advocate, Mr Ramesh Agrawal, and personally collect some legal papers.

(ii)

It was around 8:00 pm. All the staff had left, but the light in Mr Kapoor's office was still on. Prabhakar, who had just returned from the advocate's office, was curious, as Kapoor was not in the habit of working this late. When he entered, he found Mr Kapoor holding a whiskey glass. Dark circles were visible under his eyes, and he looked as though he had aged a decade in a single day.

Prabhakar couldn't gather the courage to speak for a few minutes. Kapoor looked at him, took a sip, and said, 'I've been screwed, my friend. I've been screwed. My past, which I thought was buried, has come back to bite me.'

Prabhakar: 'I don't understand, Sir.'

Kapoor: 'Remember in the morning, when I told you about my first business partnership?'

Prabhakar: 'Indeed, Sir.'

Kapoor: 'I told you how I started that partnership, but not how I ended it. My partner Sunil was a fool—I included him only because he had the capital to invest. Raghav was an opportunist, like me, but not at my level. You know everything about my business and how I run it. I've always been gutsy, rash, a risk-taker, and I never hesitated to screw anyone if it benefited me. And that's exactly what I did when I got the chance. As the business grew, I manipulated some papers and took Sunil's share through fraud. The poor guy had neither the brains nor the guts to stand against me. Without a fight, he ran away... and committed suicide. Raghav understood what had happened but kept quiet. The partnership dissolved. I took my share and started this company. Raghav went his way, but to make sure he never revealed anything, I gave him a lucrative contract from my new company—the same contract I have continued all these years. But now...'

Prabhakar, now in a trance-like state, slowly asked, 'But now what?'

Kapoor: 'Sunil has come back.'

(iii)

Prabhakar (bewildered): 'What are you talking about?'

Kapoor: 'I saw him today. He came to the office—same face, same eyes, same height. I was talking to Raghav in my cabin when I saw him standing at the door. He's come back to avenge his death. He's going to kill me. Save me, please, Prabhakar!'

Still confused, Prabhakar asked, 'But how is that possible?'

Kapoor: 'At first, I thought I was hallucinating, but then I saw Raghav's face—he was smiling. He knew I had noticed Sunil. Sunil had come with Raghav. Raghav was enjoying my misery. He left me like that, throwing the new contract on the desk. Later, I asked the receptionist—she said the man was with Raghav. I wasn't dreaming. Sunil has come back. He's reincarnated to take revenge!'

Prabhakar (calmly): 'You believe in reincarnation?'

Kapoor slowly nodded.

Prabhakar: 'Don't worry, Sir. I'll take care of everything. No harm will come to you from those people. I promise.'

Kapoor felt blood rush back into his veins. His trusted man was ready to protect him.

Prabhakar: 'Tell me one thing. If Raghav wanted to destroy you, why would he keep dealing with you for so many years?'

Kapoor: 'He must have been waiting for the right opportunity. Now that he has Sunil with him, he's ready. And a little profit along the way never hurts anyone.'

Prabhakar: 'If that's the case, how do you think they'll strike?'

Kapoor: 'I don't know—maybe they'll try to kill me.'

Prabhakar: 'Do you really think so?'

Kapoor: 'Why? What am I missing?'

Prabhakar: 'If they wanted to harm you physically, why would they reveal Sunil's existence? Wouldn't it have been easier to corner you somewhere and stab you in the back?'

A cold shiver ran down Kapoor's spine. Before he could fully process it, he muttered, 'I didn't kill him.'

Prabhakar: 'What do you mean?'

Kapoor: 'I mean I didn't kill him—he committed suicide. So maybe he doesn't want to kill me.'

Prabhakar: 'Then what do you think he wants?'

Kapoor: 'The same thing I took from him—everything. Everything I own.'

Prabhakar: 'So you believe he's after your money, not your life?'

Kapoor: 'Yes... yes, that must be it. What else would he want? That would be the perfect revenge. I didn't kill him—I took his money. He killed himself—that was his mistake. So now he'll take my money. I don't know how, but that's what he'll do.'

Prabhakar: 'So what's our next move?'

Kapoor: 'We consolidate. We move all our money out of their reach. Open the drawer of my desk and take out the diary.'

(iv)

Far from the office of Kapoor Industries, Raghav Bahal was speaking to his associate.

Raghav: 'Didn't Kapoor look like the world was ending when he saw you?'

Other man: 'Yes. I know that's why you took me to his office today. But what I don't understand is—why now? What's the plan?'

Raghav: 'I've waited a long time to settle scores with Kapoor. I stayed connected to learn his weaknesses. I even have a couple of cleaning staff on my payroll. A few days ago, while cleaning his desk, one of them found a diary in an open drawer. It had an entry about a Swiss bank account. They copied the details. Now I have everything I need. As soon as the money arrives, I'll wipe it clean.'

Other man: 'Strange that he'd keep such a diary so carelessly.'

Raghav: 'It's because the account doesn't have any money yet. Why secure it? But once he transfers funds, he'll surely take precautions.'

Other man: 'Why would he transfer money later if he hasn't done it so far?'

Raghav: 'Tell me, why does someone open a Swiss bank account?'

Other man: 'To move money there.'

Raghav: 'Then why open an account and not transfer money?'

Other man: 'Maybe it's a backup—for emergencies.'

Raghav: 'Exactly. And we just created that emergency this morning.'

(v)

A few days later, most of Kapoor's liquid assets had been

converted into cash and transferred to a Swiss bank account. Prabhakar ensured that everything was executed smoothly.

When the transfer was complete, Prabhakar entered Kapoor's office. Kapoor was unusually cheerful.

Kapoor: 'Good work. Now that we've wound up most affairs, I'll take a flight out of the country. You'll stay here, wrap up things, and then join me.'

Prabhakar: 'How do you plan to pay for your ticket, Sir?'

Kapoor: 'Good question. Since my money is abroad, I'll buy the ticket in cash. I have a couple of lakhs with me, so don't worry.'

Prabhakar: 'I would strongly advise against that, Sir—because that's all the money you have left.'

Kapoor couldn't grasp the meaning of the statement immediately. Then, raising his voice, he said, 'What the hell do you mean?'

Prabhakar: 'I mean that there isn't a single paisa in *your* Swiss account.'

Kapoor: 'How is that possible?'

Prabhakar: 'Because I didn't transfer the money to *your* account. I opened one in *my* name and transferred it there. You assumed it was going to your account—you were right that it was going to Switzerland. The only difference was—it wasn't *your* account.'

Kapoor: 'You bastard! I trusted you—and you stabbed me in the back. You teamed up with the enemy!'

Prabhakar: 'No, Kapoor. I didn't team up with the enemy. *I am the enemy. I am Sunil, you asshole.*'

Kapoor couldn't believe his ears. A stunned voice

asked, 'But how is that possible? I've known you for years—you never betrayed me. Were you waiting all this time?'

Prabhakar: 'No. I didn't remember I was Sunil in my past life. But the day Raghav came to your office, and you told me everything about how you ruined him—that's when I remembered. I was as loyal to you as a dog, until I remembered what you did to me. I thought about killing you, but then *you yourself said* the perfect punishment would be losing everything. Funny, huh? You showed me the path to cause you the maximum agony.'

A defeated Kapoor asked, 'Were you working with Raghav?'

Prabhakar: 'No. He doesn't know about me. He must be planning something else.'

Kapoor (slowly): 'Then who was that man? How did he look so much like you?'

Prabhakar: 'You don't remember, do you? When I died, I had a young son. Raghav must have taken care of him all these years.'

Kapoor (weakly): 'But you don't look like you did in your past life.'

Prabhakar: 'You watch too many Hindi movies, Kapoor. It's not a law that reincarnated people look the same. Some even change gender! Don't you know the story from the *Mahabharata*, where Ambalika became Shikhandi to take revenge?'

That was too much for Kapoor. Slowly grasping what fate had in store for him, he walked toward the open window.

10

THE MATHEMATICS OF MURDER

August 2013

Sub-Inspector Harshad Devani was slowly moving towards the office of Senior Inspector Randeep Singh. Randeep Singh was one of the most respected officers in the police force—someone who had an impeccable track record, who had cracked most of his cases during his career, who was looked upon by the newly recruited officers for mentorship, and who had an amazing story to tell from a night twelve years ago. Harshad entered Randeep Singh's office and sat opposite him. After a few pleasantries, Randeep came straight to the point.

Randeep: 'Harshad, do you know I am retiring in a few weeks?'

Harshad (curtly): 'Yes Sir, I am well aware of that.'

Randeep: 'And do you know why I have called you to my office?'

Harshad: 'Honestly, I don't know, Sir.'

Randeep took some time before replying. 'In our line of

work, we never get a 100 per cent success rate. We crack a lot of cases, we catch plenty of criminals, we get justice done most of the time. But sometimes criminals get the better of us, and some cases remain unsolved, and we slowly learn to live with that. But then there are certain cases that are thrown at us like challenges, and if we can't solve them, then we are defeated. And let me tell you something about myself—I can't accept defeat.'

By this time, Harshad had a pretty good idea of what Randeep Singh was driving at. It was a story well known to everyone in the department, but he chose to remain silent out of sheer respect.

Randeep went into a trance-like state and started narrating the incident as if it was happening right in front of him.

Randeep: 'This happened around 12 years ago. I was returning from duty one night. It was a deserted spot when I noticed a car parked in a very conspicuous manner on the opposite side of the road. Out of curiosity, I started moving towards the car when I saw a man standing outside, holding a gun. Before I could do anything, he fired at the person in the driver's seat. Without waiting, I drew my gun and fired at the gunman. He got hit in the stomach and fell to the ground. When I reached the car, I saw the man who had fired the shot—his name was Jagan Shetty, a known criminal with several charges against him. As I looked inside, I saw the man Jagan had killed—it was a well-known industrialist, Aadarsh Sethi. His family owns Sethi Industries. However, when I faced Jagan, I knew he didn't have much time. I said mockingly, 'Jagan, for years you have broken the law like you believed you were superior to it, like you would never get caught. But now look at you—you're lying on the ground like an insect, waiting for your death minutes after committing your last crime.

'Now, Jagan had a huge ego problem. He couldn't take an insult. Though he was in immense pain, he gathered his strength and replied. I still remember his last words: "You are an idiot to believe this is the last crime I've committed. Just because I am going to die doesn't mean I'm done. One more man from his family will be murdered after twelve years. Solve that, Sherlock."'

Randeep took a few seconds, trying to relive the moment.

Randeep: 'Nobody believed me. They said either I misheard him or Jagan made up a story to confuse me. But I believed him. He wasn't lying. He already had a plan in place, which started that frightful night and is supposed to culminate this year.'

Harshad: 'What do you need me to do, Sir?'

Randeep: 'Help me on this case. This is the twelfth year since that incident happened. It will be helpful to have an additional man on the case. I've already taken permission for you to join. My seniors didn't want me chasing this wild goose, but perhaps my impending retirement changed their minds.'

Harshad: 'Why me, Sir? You could have picked anybody. Nobody would have declined to work with you.'

Randeep: 'I've always liked you, Harshad. And something tells me you'll be invaluable in this investigation.'

Later That Afternoon

Randeep got his hands on the twelve-year-old case file of deceased Aadarsh Sethi. He was then the chairman of Sethi Industries, a large business house with ventures in diverse fields. He died on the night of 10 August 2001, aged 52, from a bullet wound to the chest. He was a widower and had only one son, Chirayu, aged 6 at the time of his death. Mr Sethi had four younger brothers, all working in different capacities in the company:

Name	Age (2001)	Position
Bhavesh	45	Became Chairman
Chandan	39	Production
Dinesh	37	Worker Relations
Eshwar	33	Sales & Marketing

Randeep handed the file to Harshad.

Randeep: 'I always suspected Bhavesh.'

Harshad: 'Why?'

Randeep: 'He benefited the most from his elder brother's murder. I kept him under watch for a long time, but never found anything suspicious.'

Harshad flipped through the file.

Harshad: 'Chirayu Sethi looks close to celebrating his 18th birthday this year.'

Randeep smiled. Harshad had spotted the exact concern—Aadarsh's son would become an adult in a few days. Did that have anything to do with the twelve-year remark?

Harshad asked for permission to contact the family's lawyer to check for any will or legal provisions coming into effect this year. Randeep had anticipated this and already arranged a meeting with the Sethi family's lawyers, Ram Swaroop & Associates.

He had also been following Bhavesh for a month—his suspect number one. If something was to happen, this was the time. If Chirayu's life was in danger, Randeep had to be ready.

Late Evening

Harshad was seated in the chambers of Ram Swaroop & Associates. The lawyers were unusually cooperative and provided not only a copy of the deceased's will but also supporting documents.

He knew it would be a long night. He also knew Randeep must be following Bhavesh right now. Bhavesh had an unbroken routine of a late-night drive after work. Tonight, though, he was slightly delayed due to his younger brother Chandan's birthday celebration.

The will of Aadarsh was standard. He had left everything to his son. The wealth was considerable but not worth committing two murders for and waiting twelve years.

Randeep and Harshad had high hopes from the will, but it seemed they would be disappointed. Harshad felt particularly upset that he hadn't lived up to Randeep's confidence.

Just to be sure, he went through the will a couple more times. He was about to give up when he began browsing through other legal documents, including the *Memorandum and Articles of Association* of Sethi Industries. As he glanced through them casually, his eyes suddenly widened.

Around the Same Time

Randeep was cautiously following Bhavesh in his unmarked car. Bhavesh hadn't done anything suspicious all month. Just as

Randeep was contemplating giving up, something unexpected happened.

A fast-moving car zoomed past his vehicle and rammed into the rear of Bhavesh's car, pushing it into a ditch.

Midnight

Randeep was pacing outside the operation theatre where Bhavesh was being treated. Fortunately, Randeep had reacted quickly, arranging immediate medical attention instead of chasing the attacker.

The killer had struck after twelve years as promised. But the man Randeep had suspected for twelve years wasn't the killer—he was the intended victim.

He took out his phone and saw half a dozen missed calls from Harshad. In the excitement, he hadn't noticed them. He immediately called back.

Randeep: 'Sorry, I couldn't pick up your call.' (He quickly explained the situation.) 'I couldn't follow the bastard. He ran away.'

Harshad: 'No, he didn't.'

Sometime Later

Within an hour, Harshad was sitting across from Randeep with a pile of documents.

Harshad: 'Sir, these are the legal papers of Sethi Industries. While going through them, I found a couple of interesting facts. First, the chairman must retire at the age of 60—a practice common in the government sector, but rare in private companies.'

Randeep: 'How is that relevant?'

Harshad: 'This alone isn't important, but combine it

with the second condition, and you get the clarity you've searched for all these years.'

Randeep: 'The second condition being?'

Harshad: 'A chairman must have a minimum tenure of 10 years.'

Randeep still looked puzzled. Sensing it, Harshad drew a simple age chart:

Name	Age (2001)	Age (2009)	Age (2013)
Aadarsh	52	60	64
Bhavesh	45	53	57
Chandan	39	47	51
Dinesh	37	45	49
Eshwar	33	41	45

Harshad: 'Let's combine the two facts. A chairman should retire at 60, and must be below 50 when appointed (to complete 10 years). Now, if Aadarsh had not been killed in 2001, when he was 52, he would have retired in 2009 at age 60. Who would have been the next chairman?'

Randeep: 'Certainly not Bhavesh, because by then he would have crossed the threshold of 50. Chandan would have become chairman, and retired in 2022, by which time all other brothers would have crossed 50—meaning no one else would get the chance.'

Harshad: 'Yes—and that gives Bhavesh a motive to kill Aadarsh before he turned 50. And that logic still holds *unless* Bhavesh himself was not the second person meant to be killed after twelve years.'

Randeep: 'What does that mean?'

Harshad: 'It means the real killer was willing to wait to achieve the end game—becoming chairman. Killing Aadarsh ensured Bhavesh became chairman. If Bhavesh completed his tenure, he would retire in 2016, leaving only Eshwar eligible.'

Randeep: 'So it would make sense for Eshwar to kill Aadarsh, but no sense to kill Bhavesh—he could've just waited.'

Harshad: 'Correct. And Chandan wouldn't want to kill Aadarsh either—he would've inherited the chairmanship in 2009. That leaves only Dinesh.'

Randeep: 'Dinesh.'

Harshad: 'Exactly. If nobody died, Dinesh would never become chairman. So he had Aadarsh killed using Jagan Shetty, making sure Bhavesh became chairman. Then, twelve years later, his plan was to kill Bhavesh and become the next chairman.'

Randeep: 'But why wait twelve years?'

Harshad: 'You forgot, Sir—today is Chandan's 51st birthday. Dinesh waited twelve years to make sure Chandan crossed the age of 50. Now, if Bhavesh dies, Dinesh becomes the only eligible candidate. It was perfect.'

Randeep: 'But there was another way for Dinesh. He could've spared Aadarsh, let him retire in 2009, allowed Chandan to take over, and killed him before he turned 50.'

Harshad: 'Yes, he could have. But then the police would've suspected Dinesh from the very beginning, because he stood to gain the most. By killing Aadarsh first, he diverted suspicion to Bhavesh. Since Bhavesh was innocent, you found nothing. But had you investigated Dinesh, you would have found evidence earlier, as he was the one who truly benefited. So after killing Aadarsh, he waited twelve years to eliminate Bhavesh through an "accident". If only you hadn't been challenged by Jagan's dying words, he would have gotten away with it.'

11

TRAITOR AGAIN

(i)

27/03/2020 – IIS Headquarters

D.N. Reddy, head of IIS (Indian Intelligence Section) North & West Division, was having his routine morning briefing and coffee with his boss and overall head of IIS, Retd. General Lal Krishan Malhotra. Reddy, who was in his mid-50s, was one of the top five officials of IIS. He reported directly to General Malhotra. The other three ranking officers were handling the remaining divisions and had the same rank as Reddy. Reddy and General Malhotra were joined by Senior Analyst Rajiv Tripathi, who was their most trusted officer.

IIS was formed in the aftermath of the Kargil war. The realisation that the enemy would not resort only to conventional direct conflicts and would not hesitate to facilitate other groups to infiltrate India, while pretending ignorance of such actions, was what had triggered the formation of the IIS.

The enemy's advantage was its plausible deniability in

linking itself with such actions. 'It's Al-Qaeda' or 'It's the Mujahideen, not our army,' became the constant rant of their officials.

Dayal Prasad Sharma, the then Home Minister, together with Defence Minister Rameshwar Kumar, formed an alliance and established IIS—the covert section of Indian intelligence.

RAW, Intelligence Bureau, and other intelligence agencies were efficient, but they were constrained due to constant government vigilance and bureaucratic interference.

Being government agencies, they could not resort to drastic measures, which were the need of the hour.

Someone was needed who was not afraid to get his hands dirty—to perform black ops for the government, assignments with which the Indian Government could not afford to be linked, and someone who could be easily disowned if the situation demanded.

Not the usual kind of work our current intelligence network dealt with. Thus, the agency named IIS was formed to carry out assignments without any intervention—or rather, without anyone even knowing that IIS existed.

(ii)

General Malhotra was busy on his laptop, reading the online version of *Dawn*, one of the most prominent newspapers published in Pakistan. He was interested in the classified section, which contained small advertisements.

General Malhotra had an agent in the ISI—a highly reliable one—who communicated with him through coded messages hidden in a pre-decided classified advertisement section of *Dawn*.

The General was busy deciphering today's message in the Pakistani newspaper, while Reddy was going through the headlines of an Indian newspaper.

Reddy said, 'This guy, Aniruddh Arya, keeps making waves,' then put down his newspaper on the table.

Aniruddh Arya was a young politician belonging to the ruling party; a first-time Member of Parliament with a promising future. He was known for his aggressive stance against Pakistani infiltration in Kashmir and terrorism in general.

Apparently, just the previous day, he had addressed a public gathering in the city and criticised Pakistan in every possible manner.

As per his standard protocol and habit, General Malhotra had already started building a confidential file on Aniruddh.

Rajiv Tripathi nodded slowly in agreement and said, 'Too aggressive, I'd say. His party is always looking for young blood soaked in patriotism for further advancement. My sources confirm that the high command is very interested in Aniruddh and would like to place him in a senior position as soon as they can.'

By that time, General Malhotra had deciphered the first line of the code.

General: 'We have a problem, gentlemen.'

Reddy and Rajiv sat up, fully alert.

General: 'Pakistani intelligence is going to assassinate someone on the 29th of this month — two days from now.'

It felt as though an invisible force had instantly filled the room with tension.

Reddy: 'What else do we know, General?'

General: 'It will be someone closely related to the government.'

Reddy: 'Do we have a name?'

The general hesitated before replying: 'No, Reddy, I'm afraid not.'

Rajiv: 'Anything else, Sir?'

General: 'The person designated for the task is code-named *Muntazir*. He will be arriving via Hong Kong.'

Rajiv: 'When, General? And do we have a description?'

The general waited for a few seconds as if calculating something, then replied, 'Muntazir will arrive in India via Hong Kong tomorrow afternoon. He is travelling alone, is slim, around 6 feet tall. That's all we have.'

Reddy: 'But who could be the intended target?'

Suddenly, all three men glanced toward the newspaper on the table, which contained the photograph of Aniruddh Arya addressing a large crowd.

General Malhotra left immediately for urgent work. Reddy and Rajiv were tasked with catching Muntazir the next day when his flight would land.

(iii)

28/03/2020, International Airport

Rajiv was waiting for the international flight with a team ready for any challenge.

The flight arrived, and so did all the passengers. Muntazir was not one of them. No one matched the description, and all passengers were checked, verified, and found credible.

Rajiv called Reddy: 'Sir, Muntazir is not on the flight,' and shared the details.

Reddy took a moment before replying, 'It's just a hunch, but why don't you check the footage of passengers who arrived yesterday?'

It made sense. Rajiv got to work immediately, and within an hour, identified a suspect.

The man was around 6 feet tall and had travelled alone. CCTV footage gave a partial view of him. The passport copy was retrieved, but his appearance could easily have been altered.

Rajiv sent all the information to headquarters and headed there himself.

(iv)

28/03/2020, Afternoon, IIS Headquarters

Rajiv: 'Now what do we do?'

Reddy: 'Since we couldn't catch the attacker, let's try from the other side—we should warn the intended victim.'

Rajiv: 'But how will we know who the intended target is?'

Reddy: 'We've been working on that, and to an extent, I'm positive about the target.'

'A public gathering is the most convenient place for an assassination—large crowds, security gaps, and general chaos. That's probably what the attacker has in mind.'

Rajiv looked unconvinced. Reddy noticed but continued.

'So the attempt is on 29/03/2020 — tomorrow. I collected information today about all public meetings scheduled in the city for tomorrow. There are only two prominent figures from the government addressing public gatherings. One is State Minister of Agriculture, Mr Surender Dave.'

Rajiv leaned forward. 'Who is the other one, Sir?'

Reddy gave a faint smile. 'Aniruddh Arya.'

Rajiv was now convinced.

Reddy: 'Aniruddh has strong anti-Pakistan rhetoric and is gaining immense public support. That won't sit well with our neighbours. He's our guy, Rajiv. Make sure he cancels his public appearance tomorrow.'

(v)

Rajiv's first stop was the dingy office of Mr Surender Dave. Dave was once very close to the Home Minister but had a fallout with the top brass and was demoted to State Minister of Agriculture.

Rajiv found an obese, disinterested man in his mid-60s. When Rajiv asked him to cancel his appearance, he was more than happy to comply. He wasn't even sure how many people would show up anyway.

Rajiv's second appointment was with Aniruddh Arya.

His office was well arranged and clean—an overall environment of efficiency.

Aniruddh entered the meeting room. He was around 5 feet 8 inches tall, fair, confident, and difficult to convince regarding his security.

Rajiv: 'Sir, we would like you to cancel your public meeting tomorrow.' Aniruddh slowly looked Rajiv up and down and spoke in a very slow voice, 'And why should I do that, Mr...?'

Rajiv: 'Sir, my name is not important. The fact that I am sitting in front of you without any prior appointment should tell you I am someone to be taken seriously.'

Aniruddh: 'I'm not questioning your credentials. But you need to tell me *why* I should cancel my meeting. And don't forget I'm a sitting Member of Parliament. I don't just do things because someone tells me to.'

It was a valid point, so Rajiv agreed to share the minimum required.

Rajiv: 'We have credible information that you are the intended target of an assassination attempt. We can't be 100% sure, but we believe it could happen during your public meeting tomorrow.'

Aniruddh took the advice as seriously as Indians took social distancing during the coronavirus pandemic.

Aniruddh: 'Threats are common in my profession. If I get scared every time someone wants to harm me, I would never leave my house. So thank you, but no thank you—I will go ahead with the public appearance.'

'Besides, what kind of image would it create if I stepped back due to a threat? People would call me a coward. I can't afford that.'

He was a politician after all—hyper-conscious of his public image. Even after pressing him for over an hour, Rajiv couldn't convince him to cancel the meeting.

(vi)

Rajiv called Reddy.

Rajiv: 'Sir, he's refusing to cancel the event.'

Reddy: 'Yes, these idiots always make our work harder. Okay, here's the plan: I'll send all the information to law enforcement and intelligence agencies to keep an eye on the suspect. Where's the event?'

Rajiv: 'At Army Ground in the afternoon.'

Reddy: 'Alright. We'll hand over security to local police—we don't have the manpower. You'll remain there and keep me informed of any developments.'

Rajiv: 'Okay, Sir.'

(vii)

29/03/2020, Afternoon, Army Ground

Rajiv was keeping vigil in the nearly full venue. Aniruddh's oratory skills were exemplary, but a bigger crowd meant bigger danger.

Everyone entering the venue was being frisked for weapons. Sniffer dogs had cleared the area. Rajiv should have felt somewhat relieved, but there was an uneasy feeling. Something was off, but he couldn't pinpoint what.

By the time he realised his mistake, it was too late.

A noiseless shot was fired from a sniper rifle from a nearby two-storey building, believed to be empty and secured. Rajiv watched in horror as the lifeless body of Aniruddh Arya fell onto the stage in slow motion.

As soon as Rajiv composed himself, he ran toward the building from which the shot was fired. Before he could reach, the shooter escaped in a car.

Rajiv caught a glimpse of the shooter, but he was sure—it was not Muntazir.

(viii)

29/03/2020, Evening, IIS Headquarters

The meeting was tense as expected. Rajiv was reprimanded harshly by Reddy. General Malhotra remained silent.

Rajiv took the criticism with his head down. He knew he had failed. Regardless of whether Aniruddh had ignored the warning, or whether venue security wasn't under his direct responsibility, or whether someone had failed to secure the building—it was still his failure.

But what if it wasn't incompetence? What if someone from the inside had knowingly provided access to the killer? Who could be that traitor?

(ix)

Something was still bothering Rajiv. Things weren't adding up, so he called both Aniruddh's office and the Army Ground authorities.

On a hunch, he took a big risk—he decided to follow General Malhotra.

The general left the office at his usual time of 10 pm, dismissed his driver, and began driving himself. Unknown to him, Rajiv followed from a safe distance.

General Malhotra reached an agency safe house—a place used for secret meetings or to house someone who needed to be kept away from public sight.

The general entered. Rajiv knew the entry code, but following the head of IIS into a secret location unarmed was almost treason.

It took him two minutes to decide. He followed his gut, entered the passcode, and walked in.

As soon as he entered the room, he saw General Malhotra talking to the man who had shot Aniruddh Arya.

(x)

General Malhotra looked slightly taken aback. The shooter assessed the situation. Rajiv cursed himself for entering without backup. He was unarmed, and the killer would have no hesitation in eliminating him.

To his immense relief, neither moved aggressively. General Malhotra composed himself.

General Malhotra: 'Hi Rajiv. What are you doing here? Care to join us for a drink?'

Rajiv: 'I think you know, Sir, why I'm here. Let's skip the charade—it's unbecoming.'

The general sighed. 'You're one of my best agents, Rajiv. I won't insult your intelligence. Ask what you want to.'

Rajiv: 'Today I saw this man shoot a sitting Member of Parliament, and tonight he's having a drink with you. What am I supposed to think, General?'

The general gave a faint smile. 'Okay, I'll tell you. But what gave me away? There must have been a solid reason for you to follow me. What was it?'

Rajiv: 'I spoke to several people today. Aniruddh's office told me that today's meeting was originally scheduled for 28/03/20, not 29/03/20. When I asked why it was rescheduled, they said the Army Ground became unavailable at the last moment.'

'The interesting part, General, is that when I spoke to the Army Ground authorities, I discovered it was *you* who used your influence to make the venue unavailable on 28/03/20, forcing him to move it to the 29th—the day a Pakistani agent was expected to attack someone close to the government.'

'So now let me ask you, General—why did you do that? Why did you kill a patriotic Indian? And was there ever a Muntazir?'

General Malhotra took his time as if organising his thoughts.

General: 'Before I answer your question, Rajiv, let me ask you this—how do you think we run this agency? I mean, where do we get our funding from?'

Rajiv, caught off-guard: 'I don't know, Sir.'

General: 'Good—that means our arrangement is working. Any organisation needs funding. But we are covert—our very existence is a secret. We cannot take money directly from the Government.'

'So a solution was devised. A small separate department was created—supposedly for providing agricultural subsidies to farmers, fertilisers, etc. The real purpose was to divert funds to us undetected.'

'If we had used any other prominent ministry like Defence, the diversion would have been obvious. But we needed someone trustworthy to head it.'

Rajiv now understood. 'Mr Surender Dave—the State Minister of Agriculture.'

General: 'Exactly. He took one for the team. His fallout with the Home Minister was staged so he could be placed in a low-profile position where he could operate without scrutiny.'

Rajiv: 'Okay, but where does Muntazir come into the picture? And why was Aniruddh assassinated?'

General: 'Yes, Muntazir exists. I did receive intelligence about an attack on someone close to the government on 29/03/20, and I shared that with you.

'However, when I decoded the second line, I discovered the intended target was Surender Dave. Now answer me—why would Pakistani intelligence take so much trouble to assassinate someone apparently insignificant unless...'

Rajiv: 'Unless Pakistani intelligence knew about our covert organisation—IIS—and its connection with the Agriculture Ministry.'

General: 'Atta boy. As soon as I realised that, I knew the organisation was compromised. I couldn't trust anyone—not even you or Reddy.'

'So I never told you the intended target was Dave. He was supposed to hold a public meeting on 29/03/20, where he would have been assassinated by Muntazir.'

'I gave you the correct description of Muntazir but lied about his date of arrival. I knew he would arrive on the 27th, and I wanted to catch him myself. So, I told you he'd arrive on the 28th, allowing me to go to the airport and capture him personally.'

Rajiv: 'So you were able to apprehend him?'

General: 'Yes, of course. He's in the other room of this very safe house, properly restrained. I did it with the help of Major Prakash Anand,' he said, pointing to the third man in the room—the shooter.

Major Anand nodded slowly.

Rajiv: 'Okay, so you apprehended Muntazir. That should have been the end. Where does Aniruddh come in?'

General: 'Okay, again—if Surender Dave was assassinated, what would the government do?'

Rajiv: 'They would replace him with someone reliable.'

General: 'Exactly. But that replacement couldn't be very

senior, otherwise people would question why such a small ministry was handled by someone so influential.'

Rajiv nodded. 'And that person could have been Aniruddh. My sources said he was due for promotion.'

General: 'Correct. I also maintain confidential files on prominent politicians. I can say with certainty that Aniruddh was being groomed for that position. He had already been informed about our organisation.

'And *that* was when he decided to sell the secret to Pakistani intelligence. I had been monitoring him. He received large sums into a personal offshore account, thinking no one knew. Idiot.

'At first, I thought it was just corruption—I don't care about that as long as it doesn't affect national security.

'But when I correlated the data, I realised he received the funds *just days* after he was given confidential details about our agency and the Agriculture Ministry's link.'

Rajiv: 'So, if Dave was assassinated, we would have replaced him with Aniruddh Arya—someone who'd be handling our finances, privy to all covert operations—someone already in Pakistan's pocket.

'Someone who, in public, would oppose Pakistan tooth and nail, getting called a patriot, while those bastards across the border laughed at what fools we were. Fuck.'

General Malhotra, who otherwise had a strict rule against profanity, let it slide considering the gravity of the situation.

12

TWICE

(i)

Hi, I am Pranab and this is my story:

Thirty-seven is no age to fall in love, especially when you have never done it before; lack of experience, you see. But that's just what Pranab did—ill-advised, if you ask me. Pranab was someone who had been single all his life, and mind you, not out of compulsion but by choice. He had nothing but contempt for people who were in love—'those googly-eyed bastards'.

But all this changed when he changed his profession, from a government banker to a failed share market trader to an educator; and it was there he first saw his colleague, Purvi.

(ii)

Purvi was around 26 years of age and Pranab weighed around 125 kilos; Purvi had beauty, Pranab had an inferiority complex. Purvi had options, Pranab had no choice. Pranab never had a very high opinion of himself. He never saw himself worthy of any girl's attention, especially not of beautiful ones. Make no mistake, he was an extrovert to the core, had a lot of female friends, and was extremely good company—funny, compassionate, and unimportant; someone who could be forgotten as soon as you reached home so you could talk to the actual important person in your life.

(iii)

Pranabwasasmartguy, well-respectedandintelligent, however no one ever told him the first casualty of falling in love is your IQ. Don't get me wrong—he tried to persuade himself not to get emotional, as he had done successfully in the past many times. But this time it was different. How, you ask? Well, this time the girl showed interest in him; or at least that's what he thought. His distorted worldview said that a girl may get attracted to a guy because of his intellect, his wit, his caring and charming nature. Yes, this is the exact point at which we should start laughing. But blood flows in one direction only—either to the heart or the brain; you already know in which direction it went in the case of Pranab, otherwise we wouldn't have been here listening to this story.

(iv)

People talk about 'love at first sight', but that didn't happen here. Purvi was good looking, a little bit preoccupied with herself, and most importantly, around 5 feet 6 inches tall. You will be amazed how many guys have a thing for tall girls. Pranab saw Purvi many times in the office but never felt anything besides some admiration for the way she carried herself. However, it was one fateful evening, when Pranab reached his usual cafe for his customary meeting with his friends, that he saw Purvi sitting there with her friend. Purvi was wearing a mesmerising green top, looking ravishing, and Pranab's heart skipped a beat. But it was still just a guy admiring a girl—nothing emotional about it, yet.

Pranab was accompanied by his friend Ved; Ved was someone who had recently left the company Pranab and Purvi worked for. Pranab decided not to say hello to Purvi so that he and Ved could leave the cafe undetected, because Pranab didn't want anybody in his company to know that he was still in regular touch with Ved. But the damage was already done—Pranab had started noticing Purvi.

(v)

Out of misplaced confidence in his abilities, Pranab had written a book. So, like any aspiring author, he kept pestering his friends and colleagues to read it. Many people he knew bought the book to encourage the author but had little interest in actually reading it. However, out of compulsion, Pranab kept reminding everybody—or anybody he saw—to read his book. Purvi was his daily target. He would regularly ask Purvi to read it, and she would regularly assure him that she would, but she never did. One day, Pranab was sitting in the staff room with Purvi and another colleague, Inaya.

Inaya was a completely different story in herself. She was so thin that the government had many times approached her to appear in public welfare advertisements to play a malnourished girl. Even her parents had given strict instructions not to get out of the house in moderate winds.

But she was no lesser mortal; she never considered herself

anything less than a superhero. However, the time she fell accidentally on the floor and two students had to pick her up is a completely different story. So this time Pranab shifted his attention to Inaya and started pestering her to read the book. Out of pity, Inaya started reading, and suddenly something magical happened. Watching Pranab get an audience, Purvi herself became interested, took out her copy, and told everyone present that she too was going to start reading the book on this holy day. It was the day Pranab started liking Purvi.

(**vi**)

It was a day Pranab would never forget; the day his office decided to have a party at a nearby hotel for all staff. People were visibly excited as if the concept of a party was invented on that very day. Every trivial thing was being discussed—from what the food menu would be to the appropriate attire for the evening. Pranab, on the other hand, was contemplating whether he should wash his face before going to the party or just let it be.

But there was a problem: there were supposed to be too many girls with heavy makeup and expensive dresses who would simply refuse the idea of riding two-wheelers or using public transport for obvious reasons. So arranging four-wheelers was necessary.

And that gave Pranab hope. He had a car that he could bring to the table, which could be used as a loading vehicle for at least 4 to 5 girls—his preferred passenger, obviously, was Purvi. There was just one hiccup: Purvi might show no interest whatsoever in coming with him, or the car might get filled before he could ask Purvi, and Pranab would have become a driver for nothing. Fortunately, that didn't happen. As soon as Pranab talked about picking up the assorted girls from their respective homes, Purvi was the first to book a seat. That gave Pranab hope, and it was the day Pranab fell in love with Purvi.

(vii)

For the next few days Pranab was not himself. Whenever he went to sleep, he would think of Purvi. Once, Pranab won a bet with Inaya for a sandwich, which ironically he had to buy in the end because, well… he cheated. Purvi accompanied him to the nearby sandwich shop to pick up the delivery. Then once, Purvi asked him to accompany her after office for coconut water, and that was all the evidence Pranab needed to decipher that Purvi may have fallen for him—yeah, right!

Modern problems need modern solutions; Pranab's problem was that this was a paradigm shift. He had no previous data to analyse the situation. He needed outside help. He needed direction. He needed someone to listen to him.

As luck would have it, one day as soon as Pranab left his office, he found Ved waiting for him. Ved had some legal paperwork to be done, so Pranab happily accompanied him to the notary shop. Ved was one of Pranab's closest friends, and Pranab wanted to confide his feelings for Purvi to someone. But he was afraid; Pranab was someone who was considered by everyone—including himself—to be a chronic bachelor. Someone who had never set his eyes on any girl, and was well respected for that. To say that he had fallen for a girl would alter things in ways that would never be the same again. What if he was just attracted to Purvi but felt he was in love?

Pranab thought about his image, his respect, his ideology, and then slowly said, 'Fuck all'. Never one to run away from a challenge, Pranab decided not to become a victim of his own image. How people thought about him might change, but that should not prevent him from being honest about what he was feeling now. Pranab decided to bite the bullet—he was going to tell his feelings to someone. He needed to vent; he needed support from someone who would not judge him. That someone turned out to be Ved.

Pranab: 'Ved, I want to say something.'

Ved: 'Yes, tell me.' Pranab: 'I have started liking a girl.' He said this with a lot of hesitation, trying to assess how Ved would react and what humiliation awaited him on the other side.

Ironically, Ved looked at Pranab with no judgement in his eyes and simply said, '*Shaandaar,* let's celebrate with our usual cup of tea.' Pranab was glad; he now had someone with whom he could share his feelings, without any danger of it leaking into the office.

(viii)

A few beautiful days went by without incident. Pranab started mentoring Purvi in any way he could. One day in the office, out of nowhere, a challenge was thrown at Pranab by Nabh—who would walk more steps by the end of the day?

Nabh was a very close and dear friend of Pranab, like a younger brother—someone whose life aim seemed to be challenging Pranab to reach his potential. Pranab gladly took the challenge and lost by the end of the day. But this incident set in motion something very beautiful... and tragic.

Pranab and Nabh challenged each other daily and openly in front of all the staff about who was going to walk more that day. Pranab lost consistently. But it felt good to lose—he was at least becoming health conscious, something he hadn't been for a very long time.

After a couple of days, Purvi confided in Pranab and Nabh that she too had started going for morning walks at the nearby Gayatri Mandir and asked both of them to join her in the morning. Both declined without hesitation. To wake up early in the cold weather, go for the walk, return home, get ready, and come back to work was just too much pain.

However, all this changed the very next day when Purvi shared a photo of her morning walk accompanied by a guy. That was all the motivation Pranab needed. From the next day, Pranab started waking up at 4:30 am so that he could accompany Purvi on the walk. Love is painful, man.

(ix)

The next few days were exhausting as well as beautiful. To be in the company of a girl he admired was enough for Pranab to get through his day, even if for no more than 15 minutes—because Purvi was never on time. Pranab, on the other hand, was losing at least two hours of sleep.

He looked forward every day to this alone time with her. It used to be fun most of the time, when Pranab and Purvi would tease each other about their weight loss or the type of Ayurvedic juice they were going to consume that day. But then there were days when Purvi would come to the walk with a gloomy face, and Pranab would wonder why she was so sad. The answer he got was very depressing for him—it had to be a guy.

Pranab could see Purvi enjoyed his company; he would invariably cheer her up, and in his usual ways, would ask her to accompany him to different restaurants or eateries. Purvi never said no—but then she never said yes either. Pranab was not able to understand the girl… as if you can.

(x)

One evening, Pranab took out his younger cousin Yukti for a little outing. He desperately wanted a girl's opinion on his situation, and he knew he could completely rely on Yukti's discretion.

Again, with a lot of hesitation, he managed to utter the words: 'Yukti, I have started liking a girl.'

There was astonishment and shock in her eyes—and a little bit of joy too.

Yukti: 'I am really happy for you, bhaiya.'

Pranab: 'Thanks a lot, sis.'

Yukti was genuinely happy that her brother had finally found love.

Yukti: 'I am relieved as well, bhaiya.'

Pranab was a little confused: 'Why?'

It was now Yukti's turn to be hesitant: 'Well bhaiya… how should I put it… we always had our doubts about your inclination. I am relieved because at least you like a 'girl', not a…' and she left the statement incomplete.

Pranab couldn't do anything but laugh his heart out.

(xi)

Pranab by now was becoming desperate for Purvi's attention, and whenever he got it, it was awesome. Like one evening when all the staff had left for the day and only Pranab, Purvi, and Inaya were left in the staff room.

Purvi left as usual, with all the formalities and goodbyes, while Pranab got into a debate with Inaya over some random and irrelevant issue. Unexpectedly, Purvi came back to pick up something she had left in the office by mistake, and she saw Pranab and Inaya deep in discussion.

So Purvi asked, with a hint of possessiveness, '*Chalein?*'—implying it was getting late and they should get going to their respective homes.

Mind you, there was no plan between Pranab and Purvi to go anywhere, but Pranab was still happy to comply.

(xii)

To quote Charles Dickens: '*It was the best of times; it was the worst of times.*' Best—because of Pranab's regular morning walks and meetings with Purvi and the small but precious attention he received from her. Worst—because he was still confused; he thought Purvi liked him, but he wasn't sure.

Pranab never thought he had a chance with Purvi; all he ever hoped for was to be someone who at least had some impact on her. But then sometimes there were indications—maybe purely innocent—but Pranab wanted to interpret them to his benefit.

One day Pranab got a call from his younger brother, Anadi. By now Pranab was getting comfortable sharing his feelings about Purvi with the people close to him. So he told Anadi everything about his predicament.

Pranab: 'I don't know what to do. I always get mixed signals. Sometimes I think she's into me, and other times she behaves like she wants a certain distance. I don't even know if there's someone else in her life. Should I ask her about that?'

Anadi, who was a veteran in the field of one-sided love—because for every year of his engineering course he loved a different girl, and each time it was a new type of one-sided affair—replied while recollecting relevant data:

'Bhaiya, you might not know this, but I did the same kind of stupidity with the girl I liked in my second year. I asked her about the problems she was having with her boyfriend.'

'Well, as it turned out—she became unburdened and I became burdened. I became her *kandha*. Don't repeat my mistake or you'll be friend-zoned before you know it.'

'Why the hell should we even bother if she has a guy in her life or not? *You* are interested in *her*, not in anyone else. So keep this conversation off the table.'

I must admit—this was one hell of an advice.

(xiii)

One evening, after office hours, Nabh and Pranab went for dinner at a nearby mall. While devouring *paneer kulche,* Nabh became a little emotional and told him about the girl he had become serious about.

Don't get me wrong—Nabh was someone who had a lot of 'experience' in these things, but today was different. It was the first time he spoke about any girl with Pranab and confided his true feelings.

This made Pranab emotional as well, and he too felt desperate to share his feelings. Slowly but with less hesitation than usual, he told Nabh he had fallen for a girl too.

Nabh was taken aback but recovered quickly. 'Do I know her?'

With slight reluctance, Pranab just said her name—'Purvi.'

If you could've seen the expression on Nabh's face at that moment... his mouth remained open, with the mashed paneer kulcha, and a bewildered expression.

Nabh: '*Our* Purvi?'

Pranab nodded.

(xiv)

Trust is a currency that always remains in deficit. Fortunately, that wasn't the case with Pranab. He had some amazingly reliable friends who never judged him.

Not for one second did anyone say, 'Pranab, have you ever seen the age gap between the two of you?' or 'You look like a fat chimpanzee.'

The biggest confusion Pranab faced was whether Purvi even knew about his feelings, whether he mattered at all in her life. But he never got an answer.

Now, with Nabh on his side, Pranab had a collaborator—someone who could observe things inside the office and give him an unbiased opinion.

(xv)

One Sunday morning, Pranab and Purvi decided to change their walking route and instead went to a park near a lake. It was beautiful.

Pranab always loved spending time with her—though it usually wasn't much. But today there was no hurry to reach office, so it turned out to be the longest walk they had ever taken together.

It was a leisurely winter morning and they did not realise how it turned into noon while sitting on a bench. Pranab was sitting next to Purvi, lush green grass around them, the lake in front, and warm sunlight behind their backs. It couldn't have been better.

They talked there for over an hour—about their families, their aspirations.

Pranab started narrating a scene from the movie *The American President,* where the widowed president falls for a woman and everyone becomes judgemental.

Pranab repeated one dialogue the president uses to silence the haters: 'I'm just a guy who likes a girl.'

He said these lines while expressing his own feelings, looking deep into Purvi's eyes with complete honesty. If she couldn't see his feelings now... maybe she never would.

(xvi)

During a family function in Pune, Pranab twisted his leg dancing to '*Badtameez dil*' and ended up with an injury.

He was on bed rest for a few days when Purvi came to visit him with Nabh. While leaving, she accidentally mentioned she was going to Pune to meet a guy for marriage prospects.

Pranab was heartbroken. He watched helplessly as Nabh left with Purvi, but he couldn't move a muscle. A coldness spread through his heart like never before. All the hope he had built vanished in an instant.

It took all the courage he had to call Ved. Pranab desperately needed support.

(xvii)

Purvi never bothered to call or message Pranab during her visit to Pune. He didn't even know if she had reached safely.

So even after indirectly telling him again and again that she wasn't interested in him, Pranab refused to believe it.

To his relief, Purvi returned a little disappointed from her trip. It was in bad taste—but Pranab didn't care.

The way girls treat 'nice guys' invariably depends on their own emotional situation. If things are going well in their personal lives, they respond well. If they're hurting, the nice guy becomes invisible. And the emotional pain of the nice guy? They never care. They only need him for relief when their beloved is unavailable.

Being the nice guy is never a good place to be in matters of the heart. People don't hesitate to break the heart of someone who never demanded anything. It's always the bad boys who get the girl. Always.

(xviii)

A few days after Purvi returned, their company organised a big promotional seminar. Pranab attended using crutches because of his injury. He was accompanied by his perpetual confidant, Nabh.

Pranab tried to sit beside Purvi during the seminar, but she seemed uncomfortable, and that humiliation crushed him. He excused himself and left the auditorium.

When he returned, he made sure to sit far away—next to Nabh and Inaya.

Throughout the seminar, Purvi kept looking in his direction. Pranab was confused. 'Why the hell is she looking at me now? Or is she? Maybe I *want* her to look at me.'

So he did what any normal guy would—he asked his best friend.

Pranab: 'Nabh, am I imagining this, or is Purvi looking at me?'

Nabh: 'Yes. She's looking at you.'

That statement alone made Pranab's day.

(xix)

After the seminar, Pranab invited Nabh and Inaya to his house nearby. He also asked Purvi, who gracefully declined.

While sipping tea, suddenly and out of nowhere, Nabh started recounting his love story and how he had truly started liking a girl. This made Pranab emotional too, and he softly said his usual line: 'I have also started liking a girl.'

He said it quietly so his parents in the next room wouldn't hear. But the low volume led to confusion—because the malnourished Inaya was apparently half-deaf as well. She thought Pranab was referring to *her*.

It took a lot of effort from both Pranab and Nabh to stop Inaya from screaming—because by now she was convinced she was in some kind of mini-kidnap situation.

All three laughed their hearts out when the confusion finally cleared. What did they know...

(xx)

The next day at office, Inaya and Pranab were chatting in the staff room gallery when Purvi walked in and saw them. In a very uncharacteristic move, she came closer and sat on a nearby chair—clearly wanting to listen to their conversation. Was she jealous? Even thinking that was comforting for Pranab.

(xxi)

A couple of days later, Inaya met with a minor accident and had to return to her hometown to recover. Pranab had asked Purvi to watch movies many times, and as usual, she neither said yes nor refused. Pranab had understood and never complained.

But something unexpected happened. During lunch, the staff was discussing a new movie they wanted to watch. Purvi slowly said she wanted to watch it too—and then looked at Pranab.

Pranab wasn't a fool. He caught the signal instantly. Purvi wanted to go but wanted Pranab to ask her—it shouldn't look like *her* idea.

Pranab didn't give a damn and immediately asked her out. She agreed. Pranab was thrilled—and didn't hide it. The movie was mediocre, but the evening was fabulous.

(xxii)

A few good days passed, and then things started to go downhill again.

Pranab had planned an outing to a disco for all colleagues. He especially wanted Purvi to join; she reluctantly agreed but cancelled at the last moment.

Pranab was devastated.

On the way to the disco, he asked Nabh a sensitive question.

Pranab: 'Answer honestly, Nabh... am I an old guy chasing a young girl?'

Nabh took his time before replying.

'For your whole life, you've worked in a bank dealing with people who are actually old. You've dealt with real issues. That has made you feel older than you are.

'You're going to a disco right now. You spend time with people much younger than you. None of them think of you as an "old guy". They see you as a friend. So the truth is—you're not old. You *think* you're old.'

That's what friends are for.

(xxiii)

Things improved again for a while. The morning walks continued. Pranab had started working on his physique—diet control, exercise—and had lost almost 10 kg. He even started two morning walks—one with Purvi, one with his niece Ankita.

Just when Pranab felt he had a flying chance with Purvi, something small—but significant—happened.

It had happened before—when Purvi went out of town for family functions or to meet friends. And Pranab was always the last to know. She always informed him just before boarding the train.

Today again, Purvi suddenly announced she was going to a nearby city for 'shopping'. Pranab knew that wasn't true. Even the office clerk knew about her trip beforehand.

After some digging, Pranab learned the trip wasn't for shopping—it was to meet yet another guy for matrimonial purposes.

Pranab understood if Purvi didn't have feelings for him—but he thought she considered him a friend. A friend who supported her, cheered her up when she was down. But she didn't even consider him worthy of sharing her plans with. That said a lot about his place in her life.

(xxiv)

Pranab didn't know what to do, so he called his sister Yukti.

Pranab: 'I don't know if I'm an idiot, Yukti. I have no bloody idea what's going on in Purvi's mind. I don't even know if she knows about my feelings.'

Yukti (calmly): 'You've been after her for more than six months. Girls have a sense, bhaiya. They know when someone likes them.'

Pranab: 'Is she interested in me? Am I hallucinating? Are those signals real or am I imagining them?'

Yukti: 'Every girl likes attention—even from a guy she's not interested in. She knows about your feelings. She doesn't want you to go away, but she doesn't want to be with you either.'

Pranab: 'Then why not kick me out completely? Sometimes it feels like she doesn't even consider me a friend. Just a convenience. Someone who'll be there when she needs him. Does she even care about the hurt I feel? She doesn't care about my feelings—she's just using me.'

Yukti: 'Girls are like that, bhaiya.'

Silence.

Pranab: 'Anyway… Inaya is coming back today from her hometown. I'm going to meet her in the afternoon. Maybe that'll take my mind off of this mess.'

(xxv)

Pranab reached the meeting point where he was supposed to meet Inaya. She arrived by the time he had finished his second black sugarless coffee. From a lifelong 'Teaholic' to guzzling black coffee—Pranab had indeed come a long way.

Inaya looked lovely in her casual T-shirt and jeans. She never cared about her appearance, but she looked beautiful anyway. And she looked healthy—which was unusual and borderline insulting for her lifestyle.

Inaya: 'How are you, buddy?'

Pranab: 'How do I look?'

Inaya: 'You look different from when I left.'

Pranab: 'You too—at least you're on your feet now. That's a welcome change, hahaha.'

Inaya: 'Never miss a chance to pull my leg, do you?'

Pranab: 'Never.'

Pranab had his third coffee with Inaya, and they decided to roam around the city. The two of them got along like a house on fire. Both were movie freaks who loved quoting classic dialogues. They never let each other finish their sentences; every meeting was chaos—with too much to say and too little time.

Pranab had always encouraged people around him—Purvi or anyone. Today it was Inaya. She was talented but not ambitious. That was unacceptable to Pranab, so he encouraged her through stories, anecdotes about not giving up, and taking chances.

He quoted someone great: 'It is better to aim high and miss than to aim low and hit.'

Somewhere, it registered. Inaya smiled. Pranab was glad he could make at least one girl smile. For the first time in a very long while—Pranab felt happy.

(xxvi)

Pranab took Inaya to the best cafe in the city—located on a hilltop from where the whole city was visible. Inaya, with her usual lack of exposure to anything aesthetic, was stunned by the beauty.

In his flow, Pranab said: 'I always wanted to come here with Purvi.'

Inaya: 'Purvi... so that's her name. Nice. When do I get to meet her?'

Inaya knew Pranab liked someone, but not *who*. And since she was a special kind of absent-minded, she didn't realise the Purvi in question was their *mutual* colleague.

Pranab laughed: 'You're an idiot, Inaya. How many Purvis do you think I know?'

Inaya's eyes widened. 'Our Purvi?'

Pranab nodded.

(xxvii)

Pranab went on to tell Inaya everything about his one-sided feelings for Purvi, while Inaya listened with apt attention. He ended his story with a hollow laugh; Inaya could see the sadness in his eyes.

Pranab: 'I never stood a chance with her—this I knew from the day I started loving her. But not mattering even a bit in her life is something that makes me feel like a worthless guy. Someone as undeserving as me would never have been good enough for someone as wonderful as her.'

Pranab broke eye contact with Inaya, as if trying to prevent her from looking into the heart of a man who had lost.

Inaya: 'Just to be clear—you never confessed your feelings to Purvi, did you?'

Pranab: 'No, I didn't. I thought that if I told her, she would be pissed and never want to talk to me again. So yes… I never told her anything.'

Inaya laughed a little: 'So typical of you guys.'

Pranab: 'What typical? Look at me—my age, my weight. Why in hell would a girl like her love me? Is it so wrong to be scared of losing her?'

Inaya mocked him gently: 'And look at your confidence.'

Then she continued, 'It doesn't matter, Pranab, how you look. What matters is the kind of person you are underneath. You are a guy who left a government job to pursue your interest—a job people would die for. You lost all your savings in the stock market, came near bankruptcy, yet you came out of it. You started teaching—something you always wanted—and nailed it. Your students love you. You wrote a book—bloody hell, a book!'

Inaya took a second to breathe and continued: 'Look at you now. You wake up at 4:30 am just to be with a girl for 15 minutes. You lost weight dramatically to become fitter—someone who wanted to look better for the woman he admires, even though you didn't need to. And now look at yourself in the mirror. I won't be able to tease you about your age or weight in a few months because you'll look nothing like you did a couple of months ago.'

'Pranab, a girl never gets everything she wants in one man. But you have everything. However crappy the situation was with me—and believe me, it was crappy—you made me laugh the moment I entered the office. And that is something. So Pranab, if the question is whether you deserve someone, then that's the wrong question. The real question is whether that person deserves *you*.'

'I am younger than Purvi, and I can marry you without hesitation.'

Pranab was flabbergasted. He didn't know how to respond.

He felt his self-worth restoring inside him at a frantic speed. He could feel a confidence he hadn't felt in a very long time, and a peace that had been missing for months. And for the first time in a long while, Purvi was not the first person in his thoughts.

Pranab thought, *Inaya never says anything she doesn't mean. If I'm good enough for her, I'm not that bad after all,* and smiled.

Inaya continued: 'Purvi is a wonderful girl. Look what she did to you—never in your life have you tried so hard to look better, to feel better, and to become healthier.'

Then she misquoted a memorable dialogue from *As Good As It Gets*: 'She makes you want to be a better man.'

Both Pranab and Inaya laughed.

Like a gentleman, Pranab escorted Inaya to her house. Before going inside, Inaya said, 'Today was wonderful. I really enjoyed the time we spent together. You inspired me today, as you have many times before.'

(xxviii)

The next day, since Purvi was out of town, Pranab didn't have to wake up early. Still, he went for his usual morning walk with his niece, Ankita.

But there was a big conflict inside his mind, which he couldn't help discussing with her.

Ankita was 24 and looked much younger, but she was mature beyond her years. Pranab discussed everything in his life with her, and today was no different.

Ankita: 'So what's happening, Mama?'

Pranab: 'I have no clue what's going on in my life. Till yesterday, all I could think about was Purvi, but last night I slept just fine.'

'I tried very hard—seriously very hard—to be important to her but never succeeded. I was never good enough for her. I waited for her calls but never got them. I waited for her messages but never got them.'

'I wondered daily if she knew about my feelings. Maybe she did, maybe she didn't. I believe she did. Then why didn't she say anything? Maybe she just kept playing with my feelings. What should I do, Ankita?'

Ankita replied in a serious voice: 'Mama, maybe it's time you let go of the past. You need to accept that she never loved you.'

'If she says she couldn't see you liked her, she'd be lying. You were never a priority—just an option. Someone she trusted, respected, felt secure with—but not someone she loved.'

'Everyone has problems, everyone has a past. But not looking at what's right in front of you isn't smart.'

'You are a terrific guy, Mama. Any girl would be lucky to have you. You can make a girl laugh—and believe me, not many people can do that. But you need to leave your past. You need to let go of Purvi.'

'Look at all the incidents when she showed interest in you—every time Inaya was involved. She started reading your book because Inaya was reading it. She showed possessiveness by saying *chalein* when she saw you talking to Inaya. She didn't want to sit beside you in the auditorium during the seminar, but when you sat next to Inaya, she couldn't stop staring at you. She came near the gallery because you were talking to Inaya.'

'She didn't want you for herself, but the thought of you being near someone else bothered her. Maybe she didn't do it consciously, but she did it nevertheless. So if you take my advice, you need to let go of your past and move ahead.'

Pranab stared at Ankita for a few moments before saying, 'And after all that she did to me—the pain I got—what do I do with that?'

Ankita replied in a slow but confident voice: 'Mama, can't you just tell Purvi that you forgive her for everything, say *jaa, jee le apni zindagi,* and maybe start living your own life too?'

Well, if this doesn't move you, nothing will. So Pranab decided to take Ankita's advice.

(xxix)

After dropping Ankita at her place, the first call Pranab made was to Inaya. He wanted to meet her ASAP. They met at the same cafe that served the black sugarless coffee.

Pranab: 'I want to ask something.'

Inaya: 'Yes, please ask.'

Pranab: 'Yesterday you said you could marry me. Were you just consoling a friend, or were you serious?'

Inaya: 'I'm as blunt as they come. I say what I mean.'

Pranab: 'In that case… I love you. Since last night, I haven't been able to think of anything but you. I feel a little guilty moving on so quickly from Purvi to you, but I don't give a fuck. I need to be happy in my life.'

Inaya stared at him for a while and said, 'Yesterday you inspired me a lot.'

Pranab: 'So?'

Inaya: 'You know, I'm afraid of commitments.'

Pranab smiled. 'Who knows that better than me? I'm 37 and still single. I have a much bigger phobia of commitment. But I'm not asking for promises. I love you, and I can marry you today if you want—or I can wait as long as you want. No pressure.'

Inaya: 'You told me to take a chance in life, didn't you?'

Pranab: 'Yes.'

Inaya: 'So… I decided to take a chance. I love a guy but could never express my feelings because of my commitment issues. But yesterday you inspired me—asked me to take a chance—and I'm going to do just that. Tonight, I'm going to tell that guy that I love *him*.'

Pranab kept staring at her with a blank expression. A familiar coldness re-emerged in his heart. He felt like collapsing right there, but he regrouped. He didn't know what to say, so he did the only thing he could—he repeated the immortal line from *Casablanca*: 'We'll always have Paris.'

Implying that whatever happened next, no one could take away the time he spent with her—the beautiful memories they created.

And that, guys, is how I broke my heart two days in a row.